"No man in his right mind would fall in love with me!" she replied adamantly.

He made a crazy face and gave her a robust laugh. "Who said I was sane?"

"Be serious. I appreciate you taking me to the doctor today, but we have to end this. I can't have you putting yourself on the line like this. Do you know what would have happened if my mother had seen us together? My options are few. If my parents told me to leave—"

"I told you I'd never—"

"Bart!" She grasped his wrist to show him how serious she was. "My children and I are not your responsibility! I made my choice thirteen years ago with Jake, and I'm living with that decision. You're a wonderful man. You would do the same for any Christian woman in my circumstance. That's the kind of man you are. Don't confuse sympathy with. . ." She paused awkwardly, unable to voice the word she longed to say.

"Love, Trish?"

She pressed her finger to his lips. "Don't say that word. No more discussion on this—please! Let's enjoy our lunch and go home."

JOYCE LIVINGSTON has done many things in her life (in addition to being a wife, mother of six, and grandmother to oodles of grandkids, all of whom she loves dearly). From being a television broadcaster for eighteen years, to lecturing and teaching on quilting and sewing, to writing magazine articles on a variety of subjects. She's danced with Lawrence Welk, ice-skated with a chimpanzee, had bottles broken over her head by stuntmen, interviewed hundreds of celebrities and controversial figures, and many other interesting and unusual things. But now, when she isn't off traveling to wonderful and exotic places as a part-time tour escort, her days are spent sitting in front of her computer, creating stories. She feels her writing is a ministry and a calling from God, and she hopes **Heartsong** readers will be touched and uplifted by what she writes. Joyce loves to hear from her readers and invites you to visit her on the Internet at: www.joycelivingston.com

Books by Joyce Livingston

HEARTSONG PRESENTS
HP353—Ice Castle
HP382—The Bride Wore Boots
HP437—Northern Exposure
HP482—Hand Quilted With Love
HP516—Lucy's Quilt
HP521—Be My Valentine
HP516—Lucy's Quilt
HP546—Love is Kind
HP566—The Baby Quilt
HP578—The Birthday Wish

Dandelion Bride

Joyce Livingston

Heartsong Presents

I dedicate this book to all women who have been stepped on, crushed, and trodden underfoot by those they love, yet continue to struggle against the storms of life. Even as the lowly dandelion, may you spring back and stand straight, tall, and unwavering—sustained through it all by the God who created you and loves you.

A note from the Author:
I love to hear from my readers! You may correspond with me by writing:

> **Joyce Livingston**
> **Author Relations**
> **PO Box 719**
> **Uhrichsville, OH 44683**

ISBN 1-59310-120-1

DANDELION BRIDE

Our mission is to publish and distribute inspirational products offering exceptional value and biblical encouragement to the masses.

All of the characters and events in this book are fictitious. Any resemblance to actual persons, living or dead, or to actual events is purely coincidental.

All Scripture taken from the HOLY BIBLE, NEW INTERNATIONAL VERSION®. NIV®. Copyright © 1973, 1978, 1984 by International Bible Society. Used by permission of Zondervan Publishing House. All rights reserved.

PRINTED IN THE U.S.A.

prologue

"I can't stay in Wichita another minute, Jake. It pains me to leave you, but. . ." Trish's grasp on the bouquet of pink rosebuds and baby's breath tightened. "The children and I have to go. I've done everything I could think of, but there's no other way. I never dreamed our wonderful marriage would end like this. I'd hoped we'd be together long enough to see our grandchildren."

It was a hot day, much too hot to be standing in the blazing sun, but Trish barely noticed the stifling heat, the birds flitting from tree to tree, warbling their summertime melody, or the flowers blooming profusely at her feet.

"I can't stay much longer. The children are waiting in the car, ready to go."

She nodded toward the old station wagon and offered a weak smile. "I know I haven't been the best wife, but I've tried—I've really tried, Jake. And you were a good husband. I just wish you'd been more honest with me. About our finances, I mean. I could've gone to work. Oh, I know how you felt about women working and leaving their children with a babysitter. . . ." She paused and bit at her bottom lip nervously. "But, Jake. That would've been so much better than letting our bills pile up and gambling everything away like you did! Did you really think you could win, Jake? Didn't you know the odds were against you?"

A delicate butterfly landed on a bed of marigolds, then spread its yellow spotted wings and flitted to a nearby stand of brightly colored zinnias, but it barely caught her eye.

"You gambled it all away, Jake—our house, our car, our little savings account. It's all gone. I could've forgiven you, even

5

for that, but you didn't tell me. Why didn't you tell me, Jake? Why did you let me think everything was okay? Were you protecting me? Or were you ashamed to tell me? Ashamed to let me know that you weren't the fearless knight in shining armor I'd thought you were?"

She felt a small tug on her skirt. "Mama, I have to go," a tiny, blue-eyed girl in pigtails whispered as she stood squirming beside her mother.

Trish wiped at her eyes with her sleeve and sniffled. "Go back to the car, honey. And tell your sisters Mama'll be there in a minute. I promise."

She watched as Zana padded across the freshly mown grass toward the 1985 station wagon parked on the quiet gravel road. Trish licked at her dry lips and blinked back tears of regret. As much as she hated saying these things, they had to be said. She needed to get them off her chest, for everyone's sake.

"I've come to tell you the children and I are leaving today. I'm going back to my parents, Jake." Her chest rose and fell as a deep sigh escaped her lips. "I just hope they'll take us in. We have no other choice. Thanks to your gambling, I may even have to declare bankruptcy. My father'll love to hear that! I'll have to get a job, of course, and it's gonna be tough with only a high school education and no experience. I only hope my parents'll help us. If they don't, well. . . I don't know what we'll do but somehow we'll survive."

"Mom!" Twelve-year-old Kerel honked the horn impatiently. "Please! Zana's gotta go! Hurry!"

Trish waved wearily toward her children. "One more sec, Kerel, I'm almost through." She wiped at her eyes with the back of her hand and continued. "I. . .I want you to know, Jake. I love you. I've always loved you."

A small cloud passed over the stifling brilliance of the summer sun, momentarily shadowing her as she knelt and placed the bouquet of flowers on her husband's grave.

one

Bart Ryan pulled a red bandanna from his hip pocket and wiped the sweat from his brow as a flock of Canadian geese slowly circled overhead then slid to a graceful stop on the smooth surface of the glistening pond on the Grayson estate. He leaned on the handle of his shovel and watched with fascination as the little armada moved effortlessly across the water then, one by one, they up-ended, dipping their heads beneath the surface, their tail feathers pointing skyward. He loved working outdoors like this. There was something about working by the sweat of your brow, as God said in His Word, that gave Bart a sense of euphoric satisfaction.

Bart turned at the sound of an approaching car. He shielded his eyes as the familiar limousine made its way up the long, winding lane past the tall stand of pine trees and into the mammoth circle drive in front of the Grayson mansion. The limo stopped just inches from where he was planting the new section of privet hedge. The dark glass on the rear window rolled down, and an attractive, well-groomed woman leaned out to greet him.

"Bart, as I was walking in the garden this morning I noticed there were a few dry leaves on the roses in the bed near the pool house. Please see that they're removed immediately."

Bart gave Olivia Grayson his usual smile and nod as he watched the window close and the limo proceed up to the big house. He was used to Olivia Grayson and her complaints. At least this time she'd said please. The Grayson account was his biggest. He could afford to take a little guff from the old gal once in awhile. *Yes,* he thought as he watched Martin, the butler, hurry down the porch steps to open the door for his employer, *humoring Olivia Grayson is one aspect of this contract I'll just have to live with.*

Wilmer Grayson was the most threatening aspect. Olivia was plain vanilla pudding in comparison to Wilmer. That man seemed to take delight in offending not only Bart, but also anyone in his path. Although he'd inherited the Grayson fortune from his father and grandfather before him, he'd earned the reputation of being a business scoundrel all by himself. Nearly half the residents of Cedar Ridge, Colorado, were, in one way or another, dependent upon Grayson Industries for their meat and potatoes, the clothing on their backs, and even the roof over their heads. Through direct employment and as the major client for local businesses, the diverse company heavily impacted year-end, bottom-line financial figures throughout the community's economy.

Fortunately, Bart had to have very little contact with the repugnant man, although, so far, each experience had been a negative one. He'd never understood why Grayson Industries' landscape and maintenance contract had come to Ryan Garden and Landscape in the first place, but he wasn't about to refuse it. Of course, like all of Grayson Industries' business, the contract had gone to the lowest bidder; but even at that, he knew old Wilmer Grayson could have turned down his bid if he'd wanted to.

He went back to his digging.

"Sure you're planting that deep enough?"

He knew without looking. The surly voice belonged to Wilmer Grayson. "Yes, sir, I'm sure of it."

"I don't like to pay good money to have things done a second time that could've been done right in the first place." The man leaned on his cane, his beady eyes fixed on Bart as he knelt in the flower bed at his feet. "Last gardener we had planted things too shallow. Lost too many plants."

Bart pressed the last of the rich soil around the base of the new plant and stood to his feet. At six-foot-four, he rose a good eight inches above the paunchy, balding man. "Well, you won't lose these!" he quipped with a friendly smile and a mountain of self-control. "Out for your morning walk, Mr. Grayson? Beautiful morning, isn't it?" Bart remarked, trying to be friendly.

"Too hot!"

"Ah, but it takes that good old sun to keep these flowers blooming. That's the way God intended it. It's all part of His plan." Bart brushed the loose soil from the knees of his jeans and chuckled.

Wilmer Grayson stopped moving and glared at Bart over his shoulder, like he thought the heat of the sun had affected the younger man's reasoning. "By the way, what are you doing here today anyway?"

Bart removed his gloves and snapped them against his pant leg before stuffing them into his back pocket. "Planting your hedge."

The old man rolled his eyes. "I mean, don't you have people who work for you who do this sort of thing? Do you have to do it yourself?"

Bart lifted his ball cap and ran his fingers through his unruly hair. "Two of my men are off sick with a flu bug this week, so I decided to do this planting myself. I like to be a hands-on businessman." He moved up to the man and nudged him gently with his elbow, realizing too late it was probably not a good idea. "This gives me an excuse to get outside. Besides, I like working the soil. Kinda therapeutic, know what I mean?"

"I'll be keeping an eye on those plants, and they'd better take root. Good day." Totally ignoring the question before him, the man turned on his heels and shuffled up the long drive to the house, huffing and puffing all the way.

"Yep, I'll bet you will!" Bart said aloud as he watched the man go. "I just bet you will."

&

The old station wagon chugged to a stop before the big iron gates, and there, arched over the top in big, ornate letters, were the words *Grayson House.*

Kerel Taylor lifted her head sleepily from her place in the backseat. "Whatcha stoppin' here for, Mom?"

Little Zana rubbed her sleepy eyes and stretched, her tiny face wrinkled from the folds of the blanket on which she'd been napping. "I'm thirsty."

Trish's arms circled the steering wheel as she stared dead ahead. In the distance, she could see the familiar tiled roof of the big house looming over the treetops. Even before the grounds had come into view, she'd known they would be groomed meticulously. Every tree would be trimmed, every bush symmetrical, every flower bed weeded. Things never changed at Grayson House.

Her every instinct told her to turn the old car around and get out of there as fast as she could. But where would she go? What would she live on? How could she support herself and her children? She'd barely had enough gas money to get this far.

"Are we there yet?" Kerel asked with a yawn as she nudged Kari, who was still sleeping.

Trish nodded and turned to face her little family. "Girls, remember what I told you? When we get up to the house, let me do the talking. Don't speak unless you're spoken to. Watch your manners. And please—don't pick your nose!" she added with a forced smile, trying to relieve some of the anxiety she was feeling and hoping to allay the fears of her children.

The three girls giggled.

"I mean it, girls. Your grandmother and grandfather are. . ." She hesitated, searching for words that would best describe her parents. ". . .different than most grandparents. They may not be too friendly at first." *That's an understatement,* she thought, wishing she'd had any choice but the one to return to Grayson House. "Just try to remember all the things I told you, okay?"

She shoved the gearshift into the drive position, and the car chugged up to the heavy iron gates, the speaker on the intercom just inches from her face. *What shall I say? Your wandering daughter has come home? With three grandchildren you didn't know you had? She's penniless and doesn't have a place to live? Her husband gambled away everything the family owned and then ran his car into a tree and died?*

Her hand went to her mouth as she swallowed hard and fought back tears. *I am not going to cry. I am not going to cry! I will not cry in front of my parents. They hate weaklings. I have to be strong for my children's sake.*

As she leaned out the window to press the button on the intercom, a large, four-door pickup came barreling down the lane toward her from the direction of the house, a cloud of dust whirling up behind it. It pulled to a stop on the opposite side of the gate and a nice-looking man in jeans and a red T-shirt opened the driver's door and stepped out, sporting a friendly smile.

"Comin' in?" he asked easily as he walked toward the gate.

Trish blinked her eyes and squared her chin. "Yes, would you open the gate, please?"

The man moved to the stone pillar at the side of the drive and pushed a button. "There ya go, little lady! I'll move over so you can get by." With that, he hopped back into the truck and backed it away from the gate. "Come on in," he called out the window.

The station wagon moved forward until it was even with the truck. "Thanks," Trish said with a wave of her hand, grateful she hadn't had to use the intercom to the house to gain admittance.

His suntanned arm rested in the open window as he gave the foursome in the wagon a big smile. "You're welcome. Guess I should've asked if you were robbers or something before I let you in. Old man Grayson might have my head for lettin' strangers have access to Grayson House." He scanned the car's occupants, his face still wearing its broad smile. "But I guess you don't look too dangerous." He eyed the three faces poking out the backseat's window then frowned over his smile. "You girls haven't robbed any banks lately, have you?"

Three snickers answered his question.

Trish relaxed a bit and allowed herself to return his friendly smile. "I'm their daughter."

"The Graysons'?" He straightened with a frown. "Really? I didn't know they had a daughter, other than Margaret. These your kids?"

She nodded. "Yes. I'm Trish. This is Zana, Kari, and Kerel."

"Pleased to make your acquaintance. What beautiful daughters you have. Guess that makes them old Wilmer and Olivia's grandkids. Right?" He removed his ball cap and tossed it onto the seat beside him. "Funny, in all the time I've worked for the Graysons I've never heard anyone say they had more than one daughter, and I certainly never heard about any grandkids. Guess you haven't been living around here, huh?"

She watched as he eyed the beat-up station wagon, then answered timidly, "No, I haven't."

He nudged the truck forward a few inches. "Well, guess I'll be seeing you around—if you're gonna be here for awhile. I'm Bart. Bart Ryan. My company has the landscape and maintenance contract on your parents' properties."

"I—we may be here awhile. I'm not sure. Our plans are, ah, a little up in the air right now." She nodded again. "Thanks for opening the gate. We'd better be going now."

"Nice to meet you ladies. All four of you, Mrs.—"

"Taylor. Trish Taylor."

"Will Mr. Taylor be coming soon?" he asked politely.

"No," she answered, faltering. "He—he died recently. I'm a widow."

The man blinked then stammered, "I'm really sorry, ma'am. I didn't mean—"

"You couldn't have known. Now, if you'll excuse me—"

"Of course; you ladies have a nice day."

Trish watched his truck in the rearview mirror as it passed through the gate and on down the road before slowly shifting the old car into low, putting off the inevitable as long as she could.

"Did we do good, Mama?" seven-year-old Kari asked from the backseat. "We were quiet, just like you said."

Trish smiled proudly at her trio. "You were very good. Now, let's go meet your grandparents."

❧

"Mother? I wondered where you were." A prim-looking young woman entered Olivia's bedroom without knocking. "Father has finished reading the paper. He wants us to join him in his study for tea."

Olivia Grayson touched her temples and pressed lightly with a circular motion as she answered wearily. "Margaret, please tell your father I have a headache and I'm tired. This heat is so oppressive. I must take a cool bath and have a quick nap or I simply won't be able to function the rest of the day."

"Yes, Mother. I'll tell him," Margaret answered without protest, as if she'd realized before asking that her father's request would be turned down.

Olivia watched her obedient daughter back through the bedroom door and dutifully shut it behind her. In all of Margaret's twenty-seven years she'd rarely challenged any of her mother's wishes. Funny how two daughters could be raised in the same house yet be so different. She wished her younger daughter would show a little backbone, have a little more spunk, take a little initiative, and find herself a man.

Olivia sat in front of her dresser, gazing at her reflection in the oversized beveled mirror as she pulled off her blue sapphire earrings and carelessly dropped them into the jewelry box. In some ways, Margaret resembled her. Same green eyes, same high cheekbones, same willowy figure. But that's where the resemblance ended. While Margaret would never stand out in a crowd, her mother always had, everywhere she went.

For her age, Olivia knew she was a striking woman. Nothing delighted her more than to see heads turn as she entered a room. Unlike her husband, who'd let himself grow old and paunchy, Olivia Grayson worked hard to maintain her youthful appearance. Nothing was more important to her. She thrived on self-indulgence, pampered by both wealth and an equally self-indulgent husband.

However, Wilmer Grayson's self-indulgence leaned in the opposite direction of his wife's. The man rose at six each morning and took a long, leisurely bath to soothe the ache in his lower limbs. When he was good and ready, he seated himself at the head of the magnificent cherrywood table in the oversized dining room and rang the brass bell that could always be found on the right-hand side of his napkin. As if by magic, Martin would appear, bantering the same phrase each morning—just as he had for the past twenty-five years. "Good morning, sir. And did we sleep well? And what would we like for breakfast this morning?"

Wilmer Grayson's routine never varied.

Olivia continued to gaze at her reflection as she lightly touched the smooth chignon at the nape of her neck. *I might have to find another hairdresser. My hair looks so. . .ordinary. This style is too old on me. Much too severe. I need something softer.* She separated a few wisps of her heavily tinted auburn hair from the smooth crown and tugged them down over her forehead with her perfectly manicured nails as she angled toward the mirror. *Something to make me look younger.*

She closed the jewelry box and placed it in the safe behind the lighted oil painting on the wall. Deciding it was time to call her maid to run her bath, she strode out of her room and onto the landing above the winding staircase just as the doorbell sounded.

From her vantage point at the railing, she had a perfect view of the front door and waited impatiently to see who their uninvited caller was before summoning Anna. She watched as Martin pulled the heavily carved door open, but she couldn't see who was standing on the other side until the butler opened the door wide enough to allow someone entrance. It was then she heard a familiar voice.

"Hello, Martin. It's me. Patricia. I'm home."

two

"Patricia?" Olivia gripped the railing on the landing as if steadying herself.

Trish gathered her three daughters close to her side. "Yes, Mother. It's me."

Olivia moved along the stairway, slowly lowering herself down the thickly carpeted treads, never taking her gaze off her daughter.

Oh, how Trish had dreaded this moment. In fact, if she weren't in such need and had any other place to go, or anyone else to turn to, she wouldn't be standing in her parents' house.

Martin closed the door and quickly turned his attention toward his employer. "Madam, should I call Mr. Grayson?"

"No need," a raspy male voice responded, as the head of the house moved quickly toward them, with Margaret Grayson at his side, the *tap, tap, tap* of his cane echoing down the long, marble hallway with each labored step. "I heard."

Trish searched for words but they wouldn't come. She'd rehearsed her speech a hundred times, but her mind was a total blank and her lips were frozen in place.

If she'd imagined any traces of softness on her mother's face when she'd first entered, they'd hardened as Olivia looked first to her daughter, then to the grandchildren she'd never met, and demanded in a voice as cold as ice, "What are you doing here, Patricia? Why have you come?"

"I want you to go. Now," Wilmer Grayson told his daughter, his tone harsh and unyielding. "You are not welcome in this house."

"But, Father, I—"

The man pointed his chubby finger toward the door. "Martin. Show them out."

"Are you my grandma?" wide-eyed Kari asked as she reached out and touched Olivia's sleeve.

Olivia started to speak, but stopped as she stared at the child. Trish knew Kari bore a strong resemblance to herself at that age—knew that her mother, for all her coldness, couldn't miss it.

"Mother, Father, please!" Trish pleaded, her hopes that they'd finally forgiven her fading. "We need help! There's no one else to turn to."

Olivia tilted her head arrogantly. "How about that no-good husband of yours? What'd he do, walk out on you?"

"I warned you, Patricia. You knew the consequences when you left here with that boy," her father reminded her, his tone cool enough to chill a polar bear. "Go, and take Jake's children with you—if they are Jake's children."

Patricia's heart clenched in her chest and she felt faint. She hadn't expected them to welcome her with open arms, but never did she expect they'd be this cruel. Her beautiful children—their grandchildren—deserved so much better than this. Trying to gather her composure, and summoning all the courage she could muster, she spoke, determined to hold her voice steady and not cry. "Yes, Father. These three beautiful girls *are* Jake's children. Jake may have had his faults, but he was a good husband and father. I can see I've made a terrible mistake coming here." She spun around and headed for the door, pulling her children with her.

"Stop!"

Trish felt a light touch her shoulder. It was Olivia's.

"Wilmer, at least let's hear her out," the woman said.

Margaret moved forward and spoke with harshness. "Daddy's right, Mother. Patricia knew when she left she couldn't come back."

"Be quiet, Margaret," Olivia snapped as she stepped between the two sisters. "This is between your father and me." She turned to Martin and ordered with a flip of her hand, "Take these children to the kitchen and have Hildy give them some milk or juice or something."

"Wilmer," she said firmly, turning toward her husband, "let's continue this discussion in the den."

Margaret took her father's arm to assist him, but Olivia apparently had other plans.

"No, Margaret. Your father and I will to talk to Patricia. Alone," she added with a tone that dared challenge.

Margaret glared at her mother but said nothing as she walked away with a scornful tilt of her chin.

"The den, Patricia," Olivia ordered as she led Wilmer away, leaving Trish standing on the cold marble of the foyer.

Trish waited until she was sure the children had time to reach the safety of Hildy's kitchen then followed her parents with trepidation.

"Sit down, Patricia. There, in that chair," her mother said unemotionally, as if she were talking to a stranger. "Say whatever it is you've come here to say." She moved across the plush carpeting and seated herself on the leather couch beside her husband and the two waited.

Trish looked around the room, remembering the many times she'd been pointed to that very chair and questioned and lectured by her father. *Patricia, did you break the vase? Patricia, what time did I tell you to be home? Patricia, these grades are not acceptable for a Grayson. Patricia, you must stay away from that Jake Taylor. Margaret is such an obedient child. Why can't you be more like your sister?*

"We're waiting, Patricia."

Her mother's impatient words shattered her thoughts and brought her abruptly back to the present. Trish sucked in a gasp of air and began, no longer able to prolong the agony of facing her parents with the truth.

"When we left here," she began, "we went to Wichita, Kansas, where Jake got a job as a mechanic. We rented a little house, and I know you don't believe me, but we were extremely happy. Jake was good to me. Then, Kerel was born—"

"Six months after you left here I might add!" her mother appended with a sneer that cut to the very quick of her daughter's being. "You were pregnant when you left here, I well remember."

Trish was glad God's Word came to mind before she blurted out something she'd be sorry for later. *"A gentle answer turns away wrath,"* she reminded herself before responding with calmness in her voice that surprised even her. "Yes, Mother, you're right. Six months after I left with Jake, our first daughter was born. Do you also remember you and Father gave me no other choice, except to kill my baby?" She gulped hard and straightened in her chair. "I'm just sorry you weren't there for her birth. I wouldn't have missed all the joy Kerel has brought into my life for all the wealth in the world."

Her father let out a loud harrumph. "That's good, because I told you if you left with Jake and had that baby, you'd never get a penny of Grayson money! I hope you remember that, Patricia," he retorted loudly as his accusing gaze cruelly pierced her heart. "Your mother and I disowned you, or have you forgotten?"

Trish gulped. *A gentle answer turns away wrath.* "I—I do remember, Father, and I never intended to come back. You made your position quite clear." *Although I have missed you both.*

"Then why are you here?" he demanded callously.

This was her chance to state her case. To put aside the differences she'd had with her parents over Jake and the baby she'd been carrying thirteen years ago. It was time to swallow any pride she may have left and think of her children and their welfare. If she had to eat crow, so be it. Serenely, with a voice that was unwavering, she answered, "Because I'm your daughter, Father, your flesh and blood. And my children are your grandchildren. And we need help."

The pompous man stood to his feet, his face pinched with anger. "You are not my daughter! And I have no grandchildren!" He brought his fist down hard on the desk, causing both Trish and her mother to recoil. "If you think you can come waltzing in here—"

Olivia tugged on his sleeve. "Hear her out, Wilmer. Hear her out."

"Hear her out? Why? She had her chance."

Olivia tugged on his sleeve again. "Because I asked you to."

Grateful to her mother for at least buying her a little time to explain, Trish went on, "We—Jake and I, eventually bought a little house. Then, Kari was born—she's seven now. I can't tell you how happy we were. I know you didn't like Jake, but honest, he was a good man. He worked hard and picked up overtime whenever he could so I could be a stay-at-home mom. Then, three years later, we had Zana."

Her father gave a loud snort. "So? Where is that scoundrel? Did he run off with another woman? Is that why you're here? We warned you, Patricia. But you wouldn't listen, would you? Now, you come groveling to me—"

"He's dead, Father." Voicing those words opened the floodgates of grief—floodgates Trish had guarded carefully since Jake's funeral.

Mr. and Mrs. Grayson looked quickly from one to the other, but sat silently watching as their oldest daughter's body trembled and shook as the pent-up tears spilled freely. Neither made a move to comfort or console her.

"Tha–that's why we're here," she mumbled between sobs. "Jake got into financial trouble, and the only wa–way he could think to get out was to ga–gamble our savings, to try to get enough money back to p–pay his debts. He lost heavily and put our house and ca—car up as collateral, hoping to w—win big, but he lost it all." She fished around in her purse, found a wadded up tissue, and blew her nose loudly. "He—he wanted to spare me, and he didn't tell me until it was over and everything was gone and they came to move us out."

Determined to get control of her emotions before she continued, Trish took several deep cleansing breaths and wiped at her nose with the remnants of the tissue. "Jake didn't have much insurance. Just enough to bury him and pay a few medical bills," she went on as she lowered her eyes, hating to have to explain the cause of her husband's demise. "We don't know why he didn't see the tree. They said he was doing about fifty when he hit it. He never regained consciousness."

Neither parent spoke, just sat staring at the daughter they had disowned when she was seventeen.

"He was a good man, despite what you think. We loved one another and he was a wonderful father. I—I miss him so."

"You have nothing left?" her mother asked finally. "Nothing at all?"

"I barely had enough gas money to get this far. I bought that old station wagon with what little was left after burying Jake. The remainder of the equity in our house and car wasn't enough to pay off our debts and we have no place else to go. I'd hoped, even if you couldn't forgive me, you'd find it in your hearts to help us for the sake of your grandchildren." She clasped her hands in her lap and waited for their response. This had been far more difficult than she'd imagined.

"Do you admit you made a dreadful mistake, Patricia? Leaving with that no-good Jake Taylor after we warned you you'd be disinherited?" her father asked in a way that made her think he almost took delight in her predicament, just to prove he'd been right.

Olivia put her hand on her husband's arm to stop him. "Wilmer, you and I need to discuss this. I think it would be best if Patricia went to the kitchen and had a glass of milk with the children." She nodded her head toward the door and Trish moved out quickly, grateful for a chance to get out of that room, away from her parents and their hard hearts.

ॐ

The three girls were seated around the big round table, being hovered over by Hildy, her parents' cook. Trish stood in the doorway and watched them admiringly before entering, her heart full of love for her daughters. All three were so beautiful. How could her parents refuse to acknowledge them as their grandchildren?

"Oh, Patricia," Hildy said with a smile as she crossed the room, her arms opened wide. "It's so good to have you back at Grayson House. I've missed you."

Trish threw her arms around the cook and gave her a big hug. "I've missed you, too, Hildy—you and your wonderful cooking. I've never learned to make cheesecake as good as yours."

"You always were a good talker, Patricia," the woman joked as she pushed a strand of hair from the younger woman's forehead. "And let me tell you, you should be very proud of these three girls. They look just like you, and they're so well mannered. Better'n you were when you were their age. They've hardly said a word since they've come into my kitchen."

" 'Cause Mama said we weren't supposed to talk," Kari blurted out as she nonchalantly dunked another cookie into her milk.

The two women laughed at the little girl with the mustache of white.

Hildy nodded toward the hall. "Don't imagine it was too pleasant in that den with your folks. Your old daddy can be pretty hardheaded. So can your mom."

"They hate me, Hildy. I'd hoped their hearts had softened with age. Guess I was wrong. So many times I've wanted to contact them, but I didn't. I—I just couldn't."

The two friends sat down at the table with the children, and Trish poured out her heart to the woman she'd loved since childhood. Hildy was the only one at Grayson House she could talk to, her only friend.

Martin interrupted them. "Your parents would like you to return to the den, Miss Patricia."

❧

Although Bart Ryan worked alongside his crew as they unloaded a trailer full of spreaders at the Kirkwood place, the adjoining property to Grayson House, he couldn't forget the frightened face of Trish Taylor. She'd been like a scared puppy that'd just chewed up the carpet and knew its owner was rolling up a newspaper. *So, she's old man Grayson's daughter? Her car sure didn't look like she was a Grayson. From the look on her face I'd say things weren't going well for her. She said she was a widow. Maybe that's the reason she looked distraught.* He recalled her beat-up car and snickered aloud. *No doubt old Wilmer made sure that junk heap was moved around to the back of the house pronto. No way would that man let that old clunker sit in his driveway any longer than necessary.*

"Whatcha smiling about, Bart?"

He'd been so caught up in his thoughts he hadn't noticed when Ben, the Kirkwoods' handyman, walked up beside him.

"Hey, Ben, my man, you're just the person I want to see."

Ben held his hands up and backed off. "No, you don't! You're not gettin' me to help unload that trailer on a hot day like this."

Bart wiped his brow. "Naw. Nothin' like that. I'm just curious about something. You've worked for the Kirkwoods for how many years? Fifteen? Twenty?"

"More'n that. Twenty-seven. Why?"

"Ever know the Graysons' daughter?"

Ben rubbed his chin. "Ya mean Margaret?"

"Nope. The other one. Trish."

Ben leaned forward. "Patricia? How'd you know about her? That one left a long time ago. Don't ever say her name around Grayson House. The old man'll fire you on the spot. He disowned that girl."

"Why? What could she possibly have done to deserve that kind of treatment?" He knew there had to be a story behind Trish's arrival at the mansion in that old junker.

Ben looked both ways before answering, as if to make sure none of the Kirkwood family were there to overhear him gossiping about their neighbor. "She and a kid who worked at the gas station down on Main Street was thick as fleas. He was a good kid, too. But he was from the wrong side of town, if you know what I mean. A high school dropout. Her father tried to put a stop to those two seein' each other, forbade that girl to date Jake Taylor. Well, she was a stubborn one, that girl, and too smart for her pappy. She'd leave the house with one of the other boys in town and then meet Jake. Sneaked outta the house at night even, I heard. Anyway, she's no more than seventeen when she ups and tells her folks she wants to marry Jake. Her daddy threatened to have him arrested for theft if he ever came near her again."

Bart's eyes widened. "He stole from her father?"

Ben shook his head. "Nope, but who'd take his word over Wilmer Grayson's?"

"Did she break it off? To keep him outta jail?"

Ben pulled off his cap and swatted it at a sweat bee as it buzzed around his face. "Nope, she was too crazy about the boy, and besides, she was pregnant. She told her daddy and mama she was gonna marry him and keep her baby."

Bart wiped his brow again and sat down on the edge of the trailer, his gloves in his lap. "Wow. What little I know about the Graysons, I s'pose they exploded. What happened?"

"Well, I wasn't there, but Hildy, their cook, told me all about it. She said that girl's ma and pa gave her twenty-four hours to break it off with Jake. And, get this! Have an abortion."

Bart shook his head sadly. "Some parents, huh? I take it she didn't do what they wanted her to."

"Nope, she sure didn't. Hildy said the next morning Jake came after her in his old pickup and that girl faced her parents, told them she'd never kill a baby, that she loved Jake and was leavin' with him and there was nothin' they could do about it." Ben pushed his cap back on his head and scratched his ear. "Hildy said old Grayson and his fancy wife stood there in the doorway and told that precious little girl that if she walked out that door and had that baby, to never come back. They'd disown her, and from that day on she'd no longer be their daughter. She tried to tell them they'd be sorry, that the baby she was carryin' was their grandchild. But they told her to keep walkin' and never look back, that they never wanted to see her again, and that they was cuttin' her out of the Grayson fortune."

Bart rubbed his eyes with his thumb and index finger. "So she left? Just like that? Gave up all that wealth?"

"Yep. She drove away with Jake in his old rattletrap truck. Hildy said her parents never heard from her again and they never even tried to find her. Not once. She'd embarrassed them before the whole community, and as far as they were concerned she'd never been born. And, ya know what? I liked that kid. She had spunk. Outta all them Graysons, she was the only decent one of the whole lot. Hard to believe her and that sister of hers grew up in the same house. Always wondered whatever became of her and that boy."

The two men sat silently for a long moment before Bart spoke. "She's back."

Ben turned quickly to face him. "She's back? How do you know?"

"I met her today. At Grayson's gate. I opened it for her. She really looked frightened. I wondered why; I had no idea it was anything like this."

"What she doin' back? Did she say? How'd she look? She used to be real purty. Was Jake with her?"

Bart smiled as he remembered the delicate face of Trish Taylor. "Don't know, Ben. She didn't say much, except that she was a widow."

Ben's jaw dropped. "Jake died?"

"Guess so. And from the looks of that car she was driving, things aren't goin' too well for her."

"Hmm." Ben ran his sweaty palms down the sides of his overalls. "Wonder how them Graysons greeted their prodigal daughter when she returned home? Don't suppose they killed a fatted calf."

"I wonder, too, Ben. I wonder, too."

❧

Trish moved slowly along the marble floor of the long hall and into the den where her father and mother waited. As she entered, her father gestured toward the chair where she'd been seated earlier. Once she was settled, her hands clasped in her lap, her father spoke.

"Your mother and I have discussed your situation, Patricia, and while it is against my better judgment, considering your insubordination and your disobedience, not to mention your disrespect for your parents, we are going to allow you to stay here until you figure out what to do with your life. If it were just you, we would say no. You made your decision thirteen years ago when you ran off with that boy."

"Jake, Father. His name was Jake."

"Jake," he said matter-of-factly with a scowl. "But you have children now, and while we do not claim them as our grand-children, we do acknowledge that they have material needs in their lives. And, since the Grayson Foundation contributes thousands of dollars each year to people in need, it seems only proper that we take those children in and provide for them. Temporarily, mind you."

Trish could feel a caveat coming. "And?"

"Do you remember the caretaker's cabin out behind the stable?"

She nodded, well remembering the cabin. It was one of the places she and Jake had used as a secret meeting place, though her parents had never known.

"You and the children can stay there. It's not fancy, but it's clean, and I have a feeling it's as nice as that house you lived in when you were in Wichita. We'll expect you to work for your board and keep. Hildy needs help in the kitchen; her assistant left several weeks ago. You'll be expected to put in a full forty-hour week, helping Hildy and Anna around the house wherever they need you. You and the children will take your meals in the kitchen with Hildy and the other servants, or in the cabin. I'll pay you the same wages I paid the other girl. And, without rent or food to buy, you should be able to manage nicely. Just don't come running to me for any handouts, because there won't be any."

Olivia had been silent up till now, although it was evident she'd been the overpowering influence in Wilmer's decision. "Your father is being very generous with you, Patricia."

Trish lifted her head proudly. "My children are the most important things in my life. I'll do whatever it takes to provide a home for them. The cabin will be fine. And thank you. Both of you."

Her mother leaned forward as she waved her finger in her daughter's face. "One more thing, Patricia. Apart from mealtimes, those children are to stay in the kitchen with Hildy or in the cabin. I don't want to find them elsewhere. Do you understand me? Neither your father nor I want to have them underfoot."

Trish bit her tongue. It was difficult to keep from telling them what she really thought. She wanted to tell them how much they were missing by not spending time with their grandchildren. But her needs were too great to blow them away with careless words.

"Yes, Mother. I'll do as you say."

"And, I don't want them calling me Grandmother. I'm much too young to be a grandmother. If they must speak to me, I'll expect them to call me Mrs. Grayson. The same goes for your father. He is to be called Mr. Grayson. Please make that clear to all three of those girls."

Trish knew she had to get out of that room before she exploded. She rose to her feet. "I'll make sure the children understand. You won't have any trouble with them. They're good kids."

Wilmer Grayson used his cane to pull himself to a standing position. "One more thing, Patricia. That old car of yours. . . I don't want that thing anywhere near Grayson House. There's a shed near the caretaker's cabin. Keep it parked in there, out of sight."

"I understand. I will. And, thank you."

Trish clenched her fists and gritted her teeth, knowing she had to hold on to the anger that was building inside her. "May I go now? It's been a long, hard drive. The children and I are tired. I'd like to get them settled in the cabin as soon as possible."

"Yes. Go. But, Patricia," her mother added in a tone so cool it would put frost on the trees, "do remember the rules."

ঌ

Trish parked her car in the old shed next to the caretaker's cabin as instructed. A hint of a smile curled across her lips as she slammed the door on the driver's side for the third time before it finally stayed shut. Her father had reacted to the sight of the old station wagon just as she'd expected he would.

"Well, girls, this is it. Our new home, at least for now," she said with a faux air of excitement. "Isn't this going to be fun? Our own little cabin in the woods."

"But why can't we stay in the big house with Grandma and Grandpa?" Kerel asked, her eyes big and round as she tugged her suitcase from the station wagon's rear door. "It's lots nicer than this old place."

Her mother mustered up the best smile she could. "I know, Honey. That would be nice, but we kinda came as a surprise to your grandparents. They weren't expecting us. Besides, it'll be good to be off by ourselves like this."

"But don't they love us? I thought grandmas and grandpas were supposed to love their grandkids," Kari asked with a seven-year-old's innocence as she climbed over the seat into the cargo area in search of her suitcase.

"Give them time, honey. I'm sure they'll learn to love you. It's just that they didn't know about you until today. They're not used to having children around." As Trish lifted little Zana from her car seat, she found herself wondering how her mother and father could turn their backs on these blameless grandchildren. She could understand it if they couldn't find it in their hearts to forgive her, but these precious children had done nothing to earn their displeasure. "Now, come on, girls. Help me with the suitcases. It'll be dark in a few hours, and we have much to do if we want to get settled in before bedtime."

The foursome, suitcases in hand, brushed aside the cobwebs and pushed the open the door on the musty cabin.

"Whew! It smells funny," little Zana said as she put her tiny hand over her nose and closed her eyes. "I wanna go home."

Her mother leaned against the doorway with a sigh.

"This *is* home, Zana."

three

Except for the many spiderwebs clinging precariously to the doorways and windows, the caretaker's cabin was clean. The most that was needed was some heavy dusting, a little fresh air, and a lot of sunshine filtering through its windows and doors. In the kitchen, there were adequate dishes, pots and pans, and silverware in the cabinets, and clean towels in the drawers. They even found a full bottle of liquid dish soap under the sink.

"Mama, look!" Kari called from one of the two tiny bedrooms. "Twin beds! Just like we had at home."

The excitement in Kari's voice was music to the ears of her angst-ridden mother. Trish watched as her daughters explored each nook and cranny of the caretaker's cabin and was amazed at their resiliency. To them, this was an adventure.

"Let's see how fast we can get those suitcases unpacked so we can get our beds made up," their mother challenged as she placed her hand on the old waterfall oak chest of drawers in the corner of the small room. "Kerel, you're the tallest, you take the top and third drawers. Kari, you take the second and bottom drawers."

"But, where's my bed?" Zana asked as she crawled up onto Kerel's bed and seated herself next to her big sister. "Where'm I gonna sleep?"

Trish smiled at her baby girl. "With Mama, honey. In the big bed."

A rap sounded on the outside door and Anna entered, carrying a large paper bag. "Hildy sent some nice roast beef sandwiches and some fresh fruit for you and the girls. She said to let her know if you needed anything else."

The woman placed the bags on the vinyl-covered kitchen table and backed toward the door. "Oh, and she said to not worry about helpin' with breakfast in the mornin'. You and the girls sleep in and come up to the house whenever you're ready, and she'll fix you some breakfast."

Trish quickly crossed the room and placed her hand on Anna's shoulder. "Thank you, Anna. My daughters and I appreciate the things you've brought us, and thank Hildy for me. But the girls and I don't want to be a bother, and I don't want you two getting in trouble with my parents. Please tell Hildy I'll be there by five-thirty to help her prepare breakfast for my father and mother."

"But, ma'am—"

"Anna, my father and I have come to an agreement, and I intend to fulfill my part of the bargain. Looks like you and I will be working together from now on. I hope we can be friends."

Anna looked baffled. "Sure, I guess so—"

"I'll see you at five-thirty. Now, if you don't mind, I have to finish putting the clean sheets on the beds so we can get to sleep. It's been a long day."

Late that night, Trish knelt beside her bed and thanked the Lord for getting her through one of the most difficult times of her life and asked Him to be with her during the coming months. Her life was not going to be easy. Not that she minded being a servant in her parents' house—she didn't. But being around her parents with their haughty ways and watching them ignore her children, well. . .

Sleep came easily as she turned it all over to God.

❧

When the alarm sounded at five o'clock, Trish slipped quietly out of bed, trying not to disturb Zana, who was sleeping soundly with her teddy bear tucked under her arm. She dressed, whispered a quick good-bye to sleepy-eyed Kerel, reminding her she was in charge of her two sisters for the day, and made her way across the lawn to Grayson House.

Hildy was having a cup of tea and placed her hand quickly to her heart as she caught sight of Trish. "You don't have to work today, I told Anna—"

"I know, Hildy. Anna told me." Trish crossed the kitchen, pulled a cup from the cabinet, and filled it with hot water from the teakettle on the big gas range. She selected a bag of cinnamon-flavored tea and slowly lowered it into the cup.

"This is ridiculous," Hildy said with a groan as she stared at Trish. "You're their daughter."

Trish put a comforting hand on the cook's heavy arm. "Hildy, the children and I are thankful for a place to stay and food to eat. It wasn't easy coming back and asking them for a handout."

Anna came into the kitchen wearing an early morning scowl. "Mr. Grayson wants the usual," she said sounding bored. She gave Trish a confused look. "Ah—Mrs. Taylor, did you sleep okay?"

Trish turned from pouring her father's orange juice. "Call me Trish. All my friends do, and I hope we'll be friends."

Anna took the juice glass from her hand and placed it on the tray. "Will you be having breakfast with your father?"

Trish cast a quick glance at Hildy and gave her a wink. "No, I'll be *cooking* my father's breakfast, not *eating* with him. This morning, or any morning."

Anna shook her head and seemed confused. "But, I don't understand—"

"None of us do," Hildy interjected with shrug of her broad shoulders.

"Well, you two needn't worry about it. Just treat me like you would any of the hired help. I plan to carry my share of the load," Trish stated with determination as she turned up the fire under the big iron skillet. "Over easy?" she asked Hildy. "Knowing my father, he's probably ordering the same breakfast he was when I left here. I don't suppose he's changed."

Hildy nodded. "You got that right. Nothing has changed. I hate to say it, Trish, but he's the same old know-it-all he was when I first hired on here, only worse since his health ain't been so good. I learned a long time ago to let him ramble and play like you agree with him, and he'll leave you alone."

Trish bent and kissed Hildy on the cheek. "Good old Hildy! I'm glad you didn't change; you're just as I remember you. Lovable and sweet."

Anna pointed to the woman and chuckled. "Her, sweet? You are talking about Hildy, aren't you?"

Hildy snapped Anna's seat with a flip of the dish towel she carried over her shoulder. "Okay, girls. Let's get the man's breakfast ready."

❧

Once the Graysons' breakfast was over and the kitchen was put back in order, Trish prepared a breakfast tray for her girls, then slipped out the back door and across the lawn to the caretaker's cabin. All three girls' attention was glued to the little TV set they'd brought with them from Wichita, its rabbit ears pointed up in a wide vee shape. They barely noticed when she kicked her foot against the screen door. "Breakfast! Anyone hungry?"

Trish smiled to herself as the girls eagerly downed the juice, scrambled eggs, and toast. It was nice not to have to worry where their next meal was coming from and comforting to know they'd have a roof over their heads and nutritious food in their stomachs. And, best of all, she'd be working close to them and would be available whenever they needed her. School would be starting soon and, with Kerel and Kari gone all day, caring for Zana would be a problem. But for now, things were fine. She'd deal with that later.

With a kiss to each girl's cheek, she gathered the empty dishes and returned to the kitchen.

Hildy looked up from the sink where she was peeling apples. "Get them girls fed okay?"

Trish sidled up beside her, took the knife from her hand, and began peeling the remainder of the bright green apples. "Yep, they cleaned those dishes up so well, seems a shame to waste the water and soap to wash them."

"You eat with them?"

She shook her head. "No. Wasn't hungry."

"You have to eat, Trish."

She nodded. "I know, Hildy. But my stomach felt kinda shaky this morning. I guess it's nerves from all the trauma of coming home. I'll eat later, when I feel more like it."

The morning went quickly. Trish assisted Anna with changing the bed linens and with the dusting while Hildy prepared a luncheon plate for her mother, who was the only one who would be requiring lunch.

By three, she was back at the cabin, ready to take her girls on the promised tour of the Grayson House estate.

"You mean Grandpa and Grandma own all of this?" Kerel asked as they walked through the meadow and past a vast row of pines.

"This is nice. Just like a park!" Kari quipped as she chased a long-winged bug, trying to cup it in her little hands.

The four took an overgrown path through the trees. "This was my path," Trish announced proudly as she parted the tree branches and allowed her children to duck beneath them before stooping down herself. "No one knew about it, except me. I'd bring my dolls down here and I'd play house. Maybe someday soon we can bring a picnic lunch and your dolls and spend an afternoon." She pointed overhead where the tree branches formed a massive arch. "Isn't this beautiful? Like our very own cathedral. What a wonderful place to talk to God."

All three girls tilted their heads back and gazed at the towering trees. "He won't hear us. God probably thinks we're still in Wichita," Kari stated sadly with a frown on her face.

Trish wrapped an arm about her daughter. "Of course He'll hear us. God knows exactly where we are at all times, sweetie."

Kari's face brightened. "Good, then I'll pray to God and ask Him to make our grandma and grandpa love us."

Trish laughed aloud. "Good idea." *Only God can make that miracle happen!*

"Here comes the best part!" Trish told them with excitement as she pushed between two tall pines and stepped into a clearing. "Look!"

A crystal blue pond shimmered in the sunlight, a brilliant jewel set in the emerald green of the surrounding forest.

"Is that Grandpa's, too?" Kari asked, her eyes wide with awe as she stared at the glistening pond.

"Yes, your grandfather owns this, too," her mother answered softly, her heart filled with emotion as she remembered the many wonderful times she'd had in that very spot. "But I doubt he ever sees it. Mr. Grayson is too busy with business things to appreciate the finer things of life."

"Maybe we can bring him here sometime," the little girl responded as casually as if she were talking about inviting one of her little friends. "We could show it to him."

Trish smiled ruefully. "Unfortunately, I don't think he'd be interested." Going back in her memory, she couldn't pull up a single time she'd ever visited the pond in her parents' presence. How sad to think this beautiful place existed, yet they never came to enjoy it.

"But we can come here as often as you like!" she told them with renewed enthusiasm, excited to be able to share her childhood hiding place with her daughters.

❧

The next morning, Trish had to drag herself out of bed

when the alarm sounded. She didn't feel bad, she just didn't feel good.

"You look awful." Hildy frowned and asked, "Don't you feel well?"

Trish lowered herself into a chair and rubbed her belly. "Not really, but give me a minute. I'll be okay."

"You don't look like you'll be okay," the cook added as she put her hand on her new assistant's forehead. "You'd better go back to bed."

"I can't. I've got work to do." Trish's hands grasped the table's edge as she pulled herself to a standing position. "I'm feeling a bit better already."

But not much better. The morning was agony as she dragged herself from one chore to another. And once again, she skipped breakfast.

At noon, she ate a bowl of Hildy's chicken noodle soup in the cabin with her children. She was feeling more like herself and the soup helped. By the time she got off work, she was fine and able to again romp through the meadow with her girls as she'd promised.

❧

When the alarm sounded the next day, Trish pulled herself to a sitting position, rubbed at her eyes, and stretched. What a good night's sleep she'd had, and she was eager and ready to face the day. But when she arrived in the kitchen and caught the scent of sausage frying in the big iron skillet, the queasiness of the previous day returned and her head began to spin. She pulled a bag of soda crackers from the cabinet and forced herself to eat one. She always gave soda crackers to her children when their stomachs were upset; perhaps they'd work for her. Within a half hour, she felt better.

"You can take off at noon and spend some time with them girls, Trish. Both your mama and papa are gone for the day and we've got things pretty well caught up around here."

Trish smiled gratefully. "I just might do that, Hildy."

❧

The rusty, old station wagon rumbled down the highway toward Denver. Trish watched carefully for her exit, found it, and turned off with the bumper-to-bumper traffic. She located the address she was looking for and parked in the lot across the street.

"Where are we, Mama?" Kari quizzed from her place in the backseat.

Her mother leaned her head against the torn headrest of the driver's seat and closed her eyes, preferring not to go into detail about their destination. "It's just an office, honey. Mama has business there. You girls'll have to go with me. I can't leave you in the car. Bring your book bag, Kari."

Holding hands, the four crossed the street and entered the big red brick building. Their mother seated them in the corner of a huge waiting room filled with chrome and vinyl chairs, most occupied with women reading magazines while children fidgeted beside them.

Trish stepped up to the glassed-in reception desk warily. "I'm Patricia Taylor. I phoned earlier. I have an appointment."

A long-faced woman peered over her half-glasses, ran her long, bony finger down the appointment book, then handed Trish a clipboard and pen. "Fill out these forms, please. Take this cup to the restroom and fill it with urine. Then have a seat; we'll call you."

Trish returned the cup and papers to the receptionist, then dropped into the chair next to Kerel and began thumbing through a tattered magazine someone had left on the table. Forty-five minutes later, the door opened and Patricia's name was called out loudly.

Trish quickly dropped the magazine—the third one she'd leafed through with unseeing eyes—and moved toward the open door after a few last-minute instructions to Kerel about watching her sisters while she was gone.

The lady showed her to a cubicle, and minutes later, a pleasant woman in a white medical coat moved briskly into the room. "Hello, Mrs. Taylor. I'm Dr. Brewer. How are you today?"

Trish managed a weak smile. "Fine, thank you."

"So," the doctor asked, "you think you might be pregnant, huh?"

Trish nodded.

"Well, let's have a look."

Dr. Brewer reviewed test results and asked a few questions about her cycle. "I'd say you're about nine weeks along."

Trish held her breath. Her life was complicated enough without this. "Are you sure? Could you have made a mistake?"

The woman scribbled on the clipboard while she talked. "No, no mistake. I hope this isn't bad news for you."

"No. Well, yes. What I mean is—I'm a widow. My husband died in an automobile accident a few weeks ago."

The doctor put her hand on Trish's arm reassuringly. "I'm so sorry."

"I—ah, I loved my husband, and under any other circumstances, I'd be thrilled to hear I'm pregnant, but just not now. I have three children to support, and I don't know how I'm going to be able to work with. . ."

The doctor smiled and gave her a hug. "Now, don't you worry. If it's finances you're worrying about, remember we're a free clinic. If you don't have the money to pay for our services, it's okay. You and your baby will get wonderful care here."

Trish twisted the hem of her shirt between her fingers. "You don't know how glad I am to hear that."

"Promise me you'll take care of yourself, and we'll do the rest."

Thank You, Lord.

The four arrived back at Grayson House in time for the girls' favorite cartoon show. After a quick word to Kerel, Trish headed down the path behind the shed toward the grove of trees beyond the fence, leaving her daughters behind. She needed to be alone. She pushed through a rickety gate, half hidden by dense trees, and continued on an overgrown path to a small clearing by a rapidly moving stream. There, at the opposite edge of the clearing, was a gazebo, long ago abandoned by the early members of the Grayson family, now nearly covered by vines and overgrowth. But she remembered it well. It, too, had served as a meeting place for her and Jake, at the furthermost corner of the Grayson estate.

Trish brushed away the webs from the latticework, and debris and leaves from the bench, before seating herself. "Pregnant! I'm pregnant!" she cried out to the forest surrounding her. For the first time in weeks, she was totally alone. There was no one to hear her, no one for whom to put up a brave front.

"Pregnant! Pregnant! Pregnant!" she shouted with all her might, her fists clenched, and then began to cry. Softly, at first, but as her anxiety began to build, her sobs became almost overwhelming as her heart spilled over and the words gushed forth. "God! Why? How much can I take? Have You forsaken me? Have You forgotten me? Are You punishing me for defying my parents all those years ago and leaving with Jake?" She rose to her feet and lifted both hands heavenward, tears rolling down her cheeks in torrents. "Have You brought me this far only to abandon me?"

"No, don't ever think that!" a baritone voice boomed out.

four

She turned, startled, her hand over her heart.

"I'm sorry, I didn't mean to eavesdrop," Bart Ryan explained as he moved quickly up the steps of the gazebo. "Are you okay? I heard you crying." He seemed embarrassed but genuinely concerned. "Can I help?"

Trish turned away and blotted at her eyes with her sleeve. "I—I'm fine. Just leave me alone, please."

"You're not fine. Anyone could see that." He gently touched her shoulder. "Look, I'll leave if you want me to, but I think what you need right now is a friend." He continued to let his hand rest on her shoulder, and when she didn't pull away from him, he moved around in front of her. "Please. Let me help," he whispered as he warily slipped an arm about her waist and drew her to him. "I think what you need is a shoulder to cry on."

She wanted to push him away, to tell him it was none of his business and he had no right to intrude upon her like this. But she couldn't. He was right. She did need a friend, someone to talk to. And here he was, willing and available.

"Go on. Let it all out," he encouraged as he wrapped her in his long arms and cupped her head against his chest. "Cry, little lady. It'll make you feel better."

It felt good to be held again. She missed being wrapped in the safety of Jake's embrace. Even after she'd found out he'd gambled their holdings away, she still felt safe in her husband's arms. He'd promised to take care of her 'til death do they part and she'd never doubted his promise. She would never believe he had taken his own life, despite what the police report said.

She cried until she could cry no more, then lifted misty eyes to his and murmured, "I'm sorry. I shouldn't ha—"

He tightened his grip around her waist and, with his thumb, wiped the tears from her cheeks. "Shh. Don't apologize. I told you to cry. Remember?" His gentle smile was like a soothing salve on an open wound. "Just relax, okay?" Once more he cupped her head in his hand and rested it against him. No questions. No condemnation.

She closed her eyes and leaned into him, relishing each comforting moment. The sounds of the forest surrounded them as birds flitted from branch to branch, calling out to one another, and the brook babbled as it spilled over the rocks and ridges of the winding stream. Occasionally, Trish sighed deeply as she allowed herself to be held in the arms of a stranger.

Despite the comfort of his embrace and the longing to stay there forever rather than face her difficulties, she forced herself to push away and asked, "How did you know I was here?"

He dropped onto the weathered seat and tugged on her hand. "Know? I didn't know you were here until I heard you shout something. I was repairing the Kirkwoods' fence along the property line between the two estates when I heard you and came to see what was wrong. I didn't know it was you until I scaled the fence and came running."

"Did you. . . ?" She lowered her head to avert his compassionate brown eyes.

"Hear what you said? Yes, I heard," he confessed as his hand sought hers.

"Then you know—"

"You're pregnant? Yes. I know."

Trish reared back, pulling her hand from his grasp. "You won't tell anyone, will you?" The thought of her news getting out before she had a chance to map out a plan frightened her. This was almost déjà vu. She was pregnant with Jake's child when she left thirteen years ago. And here she was, back again—and pregnant once again with his child. Only this time, Jake wasn't there to help.

Bart gave her a reassuring smile as he placed his hand over his heart. "I won't tell a soul."

"Well," she began, filled with trust for this stranger who'd entered her life so unexpectedly. "I guess under the circumstances, you deserve to know all the gory details of Patricia Grayson Taylor's life."

As the two sat together, she explained how her parents had forbidden her to date Jake Taylor because he wasn't good enough to date a Grayson and how she'd defied them. "I wasn't a rebel, Bart. Honest. Jake was a good kid. Everyone liked him. And yes, he dropped out of school the summer of his junior year, but what choice did he have? His dad left his mom and, on her waitress salary, she couldn't afford to keep a roof over their heads. He had to quit and go to work and help her with the finances. I admired him for it. Otherwise, they might've had to go on welfare, and Jake would never do that, not as long as he was able to work. He was a fine, honorable man. Ask anyone who knew him, except my dad."

"I've heard it already," he confided. "My friend Ben, the Kirkwoods' handyman, told me. He said Jake was a great kid, and so were you."

She allowed a heavy sigh to escape her lips and shifted her position on the gazebo's seat, then recounted how she'd left home, pregnant, thirteen years ago to marry Jake because she wouldn't have the abortion her parents demanded.

"I could never have an abortion, Bart. Not then." She glanced down as she placed her hand on her abdomen. "Not now."

Bart's brow knitted into a heavy frown. "You think they'll want you to have an abortion when they find out about this baby?"

"That or they'll send me on my way." She went on to

explain how her parents had disinherited her and refused to acknowledge her as their daughter.

"What about those beautiful daughters of yours? Surely they'll want you to stay because of them."

She blinked hard. While it hurt to talk about it, she was grateful for someone in whom to confide. "They not only don't acknowledge them as their grandchildren, they've made it perfectly clear the house is off-limits to them. My girls are just a philanthropic project to my parents. I'm to work for our board and keep and otherwise stay out of sight. We live in the caretaker's cabin."

"Amazing." Bart shook his head and patted her hand. "Oh, Trish, I'm so sorry."

"So you can see why the news of this pregnancy pushed me over the edge, can't you?"

A slight smile curled at his lips. "Yes, of course, I can. But didn't I also hear you cry out to God?"

Her heart clenched within her as she remembered her outburst and she answered shyly, "Yes. I did."

"Does that mean you're a Christian?"

Her face brightened. "Yes! Are you? A Christian, I mean? I confessed my sins and accepted the Lord at the church in Wichita where Jake and I attended."

Bart stood straight and tall and answered proudly, "I sure am. Since I was a teenager."

This was too good to be true. The hardest part of leaving Wichita was leaving her Christian friends behind and the church she loved. Her church friends had rallied around her and the children as soon as word of Jake's accident hit the television news and were there for her, providing shoulders to lean on, as well as food, encouragement, and in many other ways too numerous to count. But she didn't expect them to support her or cover her remaining debt, so she had reluctantly come back to Grayson House.

"Oh, Bart," she exclaimed with renewed joy as she looked into his ruddy face. "Surely God has sent you to me." Her enthusiasm soured quickly as reality set in. "But you must never let my parents know we're friends. They'll turn on you. I know it. They'd take their business away from you in a nanosecond if they ever found out you befriended me. I'd never be able to forgive myself."

"Well, perhaps if they don't see us together, they won't realize we're friends."

"But if they do," she cautioned, "we must tell them the truth. I won't lie to them, and I won't put you in that position, either."

"I've taught my boys lying is a sin and God hates a liar. As much as I'd like to protect our friendship, I would never lie about it. And I won't be running to your parents with a news flash—that's none of my business."

Trish had to smile. "Makes sense. My girls rarely come in contact with their grandparents, so I doubt they'll have an opportunity to ever mention your name around them."

He grinned. "Same with my boys. I'm not sure they've ever seen the Graysons."

"How many boys do you have?"

"Three. That's another thing we have in common. Single parents of three kids."

"Oh! I have to get back. The girls are probably wondering where I am."

He reached into his pocket and drew out his business card, then lifted her hand and brushed his lips across it gallantly. "I'll be praying for you, fair lady. But promise me. When you need a friend, give me a call and I'll meet you right here in this gazebo. I want to help, Trish, if you'll let me."

She backed away and down the steps. "Thanks. You may be sorry you offered!" With that, she turned and hurried back up the trail.

The three girls were sitting on the porch when their mother appeared around the shed. "Mom! Where were you?" Kerel asked with a look of concern etched on her face.

"Sorry, honey. I didn't think I'd be gone that long. I just needed to be alone for awhile. I had some things to think over. Is your TV program over?"

Kerel rolled her eyes. "Hours ago!"

Trish smiled at her eldest daughter. "Now, Kerel, you wouldn't exaggerate, would you? *Hours* ago?"

She'd been debating all afternoon about when she should tell the girls about the new addition that would be arriving at the beginning of the year, and had decided that for now, anyway, she would keep it to herself. If the medication Dr. Brewer had given her worked, maybe no one would suspect for a little while—at least until it became necessary for her to wear maternity clothes.

"Let's go up to the house, and I'll fix you some supper, okay?"

❧

The pills kept her nausea to a minimum the next morning. At three, Trish folded her apron, said good-bye to Hildy, and with the picnic hamper she'd prepared for her family's supper, she headed toward the caretaker's cabin. Her shoulders sagged as she moved across the lawn. What would her mother say if she knew she was pregnant? How long could Trish keep it a secret? So caught up in her thoughts was she that she didn't hear the pickup truck as it slowly rolled up beside her.

"Hey, lady," Bart called out, his long neck craning out the window on the driver's side. "Need a ride?"

Trish stopped in her tracks. "Oh, Bart! Don't stop. Please, keep away from me."

"But I—"

She waved her arm to motion him on. "Just go. Please!"

"Only if you'll meet me later. Say about six o'clock, at our place," he said with a wink. "Okay?"

She wanted to say no. Causing Bart trouble was the last thing she wanted to do. He'd been so kind to her. But no doubt he wouldn't leave until she agreed to meet him. "Okay. But leave, please. Before it's too late."

She watched as the pickup moved up the road past the main house and disappeared. As far as she could tell, their chance meeting had gone undetected.

After their early supper, she and her three children walked hand in hand across the meadow and through the trees, to their final destination—the old gazebo.

❧

Bart seated himself atop the picnic table, one booted foot resting on the bench. He hadn't been able to get Trish Taylor's sad expression off his mind. As a Christian, he was obliged to help the widows and orphans. And, as a deacon in his church he had, many times. But those times, he'd done it as a member of the church board. This time it was different. God had placed this widow and her children directly in his path.

His thoughts were interrupted abruptly as Trish and her girls stepped through the break in the trees and into the small clearing. He jumped to his feet and rushed to meet them.

"Hi, Bart," she said, greeting him almost shyly. "Your boys?"

"Hi, Trish," he responded with a burst of pride as he nodded toward his sons, who were tossing a football back and forth. "Yep, all three of those handsome rascals." He motioned to his boys, who dropped their ball and hurried to his side. His hand moved to each boy's shoulder as he introduced him. "Andy's four, Kyle's eight, and Zeb is sixteen."

Each boy smiled and nodded in turn.

"Boys," Bart said, moving to the Taylor family, "this is Mrs. Taylor, and—let me see—" Grinning, he eyed the three girls before continuing. "I met these lovely young ladies when they arrived at Grayson House, but I've forgotten who's who!" He gave a slight chuckle and turned to their mother. "Help me, Mama."

Trish blushed slightly. "Kerel, twelve. Kari, seven. And Zana, four." She nodded toward the boys. "Nice to meet you, Andy, Kyle, and Zeb." She stood awkwardly, as if unsure what should happen next.

Bart took the lead. "Girls, guess what the boys and I found? A bird's nest! Wanna see it?"

"I'll show 'em, Dad," Kyle volunteered as he motioned for them to follow him. "Come on, it's over this way."

Trish nodded her approval and the two sets of children headed off through the trees, leaving the two adults alone.

Bart took Trish's hand, pulled her toward the seat in the old gazebo, and sat down. "Now, tell me, did something upset you today?"

She took a deep breath. "Nothing specific. I just don't know what to do, Bart. Oh, I don't mean I can't take whatever they dish out; I can. And will! I guess right now my hormones are getting the best of me. Pregnancy does funny things to a woman," she added with a slight smile.

Bart patted her hand knowingly. "How well I remember. My late wife went through the same thing with each of the boys. It did strange things to her emotions, too. But you can only take so much. Wish there was some way I could help."

Trish looked up at him and said sincerely, "You already are. Just having someone to talk to really helps. Being able to unload on you makes me feel better somehow."

He brushed a lock of hair from her forehead and gazed into the blueness of her sad eyes. She was so young, so lovely, and to have to go through such demeaning treatment. . . And, as if the loss of her husband and the horrendous time her parents were putting her though weren't enough, she was pregnant with her late husband's child. His heart went out to her and he wanted to help, to somehow ease her pain, but how could he? Especially without jeopardizing his own position with her parents?

"Tell me about her, Bart—your wife." She pulled away from him slightly with a motherly glance toward her children, who were standing mesmerized as Kyle and Zeb skipped stones across the stream. "I mean—what was she like?"

Bart leaned back on the rustic bench and stuck his long legs straight out in front of him, feeling totally comfortable with this woman he barely knew.

"Well," he began, "Charlotte was just about the prettiest gal around. We went to high school together, got married, and she worked so I could get my college degree. The Christmas after my graduation, Zeb was born and she became the stay-at-home mom she'd always wanted to be. She was not only my wife—and the love of my life—she was my best friend. It nearly killed me when I lost her." He shoved his hands deep into his pockets and turned his head away from her in the pretense of looking at the children, the loss of his wife still causing an ache around his heart.

Trish patted his shoulder as if to console him. "Oh, Bart, I wish I could've known her. How long has it been?"

Bart cleared his throat and swallowed, hoping his voice wouldn't crack with emotion. "She died in childbirth when Andy was born," he explained in an almost whisper.

"Oh, I'm so sorry."

He blinked hard. "I sure wasn't prepared for it. It'd been such a happy time for both of us. We'd wanted a little girl, and I, kiddingly, told her I was gonna trade her in for another woman if she didn't produce a girl." Bart straightened awkwardly in the seat and crossed his ankles. "They let me stay in the delivery room. When little Andy made his appearance, I kissed her and told her another boy was just fine with me." His brow unfurled and a smile formed slowly. "I told her we could have a girl the next time. She pulled a face and declared loudly, 'Who says there'll be a next time?' "

He felt his face cloud up once more. "She was right. There never would be a next time."

Trish frowned.

"Well," Bart continued, "I cut the umbilical cord, then the doctor placed little Andrew in my arms and I carried him over to the scales. Next thing I knew, the delivery room staff went into a panic and the nurses were shoving me out the door. All I remember hearing was the doctor's voice shouting, 'We got big trouble,' as the door shut behind me."

The young mother closed her eyes as if she were feeling the pain as Bart relayed the loss of his wife.

"I never felt so alone in my life. Not knowing was the worst part. It seemed like an eternity before the doctor came out of that room, but when he did, I knew from the look on his face she was gone." He bent forward, his elbows resting on his knees, his head in his hands, his shoulders hunched.

Trish's hand came to rest softly on his shoulder, her fingers lightly kneading his tight muscles. The two sat silently, in stark contrast to the sounds of glee coming from the stream as Zeb and Kyle continued pelting the water with the stones, showing off for the girls.

Suddenly, Bart stood to his feet, a broad smile on his face as he snatched both of Trish's hands in his. "Hey, lady, I invited you here so I could cheer you up and look what I've gone and done! Let's put on our best smiles and go see what our kids are up to, okay?"

Trish returned his smile and the two strolled toward the stream.

"Look, Mama," little Zana cried out as the two approached. "Me and Andy are throwing rocks. Zeb said we could."

Trish looked from Zana to Bart. "Looks like our kids are hitting it off."

"I knew they would. Hey, girls, if you think my boys are

good at skipping rocks, watch this," he boasted as he gathered a handful of stones.

"Aw, Dad," Zeb complained with a grin, his hands on his hips. "That's not fair. You been doin' it since you came across Colorado in a covered wagon!"

"Outta my way, boy," Bart cajoled as he playfully shoved his eldest son to one side. "Just watch this old-timer! I can get at least ten skips outta this old rock."

Trish moved up beside Bart as he surveyed the rock then the stream. "You can do it, Bart. I know you can," she told him as she clapped her hands, her laughter filling the air.

"How about a kiss for good luck?" he asked mischievously.

"The rock or you, Dad?" Zeb teased as he watched his father with obvious admiration.

Bart shook his fist at his son. "The rock, you goofball!"

Trish gave Zeb a pouting look. "Aw, I was gonna kiss your dad. I'm not real keen on kissin' rocks."

Bart encircled her waist with his free arm and pulled her to him as he turned his head and offered his cheek. "Then, put her there, little lady!"

Standing on tiptoes, she planted a kiss on his freshly shaven face with a girlish giggle. "Show these youngsters how we did it in the olden days."

Dropping his hold on her, he moved to the edge of the stream once more, eyed it as carefully as a land surveyor would through a transit, wound up, and let the rock fly with a sideways thrust of his arm.

The group counted aloud as it skimmed across the water. "Five. Six. Seven. Eight. Nine. Ten. Eleven! Yea!"

"You did it!" Trish shouted triumphantly as she jumped into Bart's open arms, her hands linking behind his neck.

He lifted her off the ground and twirled her in circles as they laughed together. "Guess I showed them whippersnappers!" he bragged as he hugged her to him.

"I'll bet Zeb can get twelve!" Kerel challenged as she moved to stand next to the teenager.

"Me, too," Kari added as she hurried to his other side.

Zeb grinned.

"What?" Bart asked with a mock frown. "You girls think my son can outdo me?" He reached down and picked Zana up in one arm and Andy in the other. "How about you two? Do you think Zeb can beat me?"

Zana buried her face in his neck shyly, but Andy spoke up boldly. "No one can beat my daddy!" he declared confidently.

"Okay, Zeb," Bart challenged as he held the two small children. "Do your stuff. But you only get one chance. Make it a good one!"

The happy group gathered around the boy, watching as he carefully selected just the right rock, tried it out for weight, and raised his arm to throw.

"Wait!" Bart quickly set Andy and Zana down then grabbed Trish's hand and tugged her toward his son. "I don't want you claiming I had any unfair advantage. Let Trish kiss your cheek for good luck!"

Trish wrapped the young man in her arms and dramatically planted a big kiss on his face. "Now, see if you can beat your dad," she said, grinning.

Zeb's eyes sparkled as he gave full attention to his mission. The stone left his hand at just the right second and flew through the air, right on track, as the group counted in unison.

"Four. Five. Six. Seven. Eight. Nine. Ten—oh, no!"

Bart jumped forward to shake his son's hand. "Pretty good, I'd say. Not many people, aside from old-timers like your old pa, can get ten skips. I congratulate you," he said proudly as he hugged his son.

Zeb threw his arms around his father and the two men stood hugging and laughing. "With a little more practice, I'll getcha, Dad," the boy cautioned good-naturedly.

The group made their way back to the gazebo where Bart had placed a cooler filled with ice and soda pop.

After making sure everyone had his drink of choice, he dropped onto the gazebo bench beside Trish. "You gonna be okay, little lady?" he asked with true concern. "I mean, with the kind of treatment your mom and pop are givin' ya?"

She took a slow sip. "Sure, with a friend like you!" she declared as she looked into his eyes. "Thanks, Bart. This evening with you and the boys has been the best I've had in a long time."

"Hey, I unloaded on you! Remember? Sorry, I didn't mean to get so gloomy on you, talkin' about Charlotte like I did. It's just you're so easy to talk to—and you understand, losing your husband like you did."

She placed her hand on his arm and lifted her chin. "Because of you, Bart, I know I can face whatever the future holds. You've made it, raising three fine boys by yourself. Surely I can do the same for my girls—with God's help!"

"You sure can, little lady. I'm so thankful He's promised to be with us. Can't tell you how many times I felt like quittin', but His Word encouraged me and kept me goin'. That—and prayer!"

Trish let out a big sigh. "Wish my folks knew Him. I can't even say the name Jesus without them coming apart! The last thing they want in their life is *religion*. Especially my kind of religion!"

"We'll just have to pray them into the Kingdom, Trish. Nothing is impossible with God." His gaze locked with the young mother's. They had so much in common. Each had lost a spouse through death. Each had three children they were raising alone. And, best of all, both of them loved the Lord. It felt good to sit beside her, talking about their lives and loves. Despite his vow to never marry again, and never wanting to be in a position of loving someone so much he wanted to die when separated from her, he found himself enjoying Trish's company a little more than he had intended.

"Thank you for a lovely evening, Bart—and Zeb and Kyle and Andy, but we must be getting back. It's nearly dark and I didn't leave any lights on."

"At least let us men walk you ladies to the clearing," Bart offered gallantly as he and the boys began to move alongside Trish and her family.

When they reached the clearing, Bart took both Trish's hands in his. "Sleep well, little one. And remember, when counting sheep doesn't work—talk to the Shepherd," he added as he said a reluctant good-bye. "Remember, Trish. I'm as close as the phone. When things get rough, tell God. Then, tell me and I'll come running!"

࿎

Trish, Zana, Kari, and Kerel held hands as they crossed the meadow.

"Oh, no!" Trish cried aloud as they rounded the old shed near the caretaker's cabin. "Someone has turned on the lights in our house!"

five

"You girls wait here in the yard while I check out the house," Trish instructed, her heart pounding with expectancy as she positioned them behind a big tree, hoping if there were intruders in the cabin they'd think she was alone.

She pulled the screen door open as quietly as she could and moved in silently. The tiny living room was exactly as she'd left it, except for the light now burning brightly on the end table. She cautiously crossed the room and went into the kitchen where she found the light lit over the round table in the corner. Then she spotted it! A note propped up against the salt and pepper shakers in Hildy's handwriting, telling her she didn't have to come in early in the morning. Her parents had left town on an unexpected business trip and wouldn't be back until after the weekend. It also said she'd left the lights on, assuming they were taking an evening walk and would be home soon.

Trish's breathing returned to normal.

Once the girls were tucked into bed, she read her Bible and soon fell into a restful sleep, only to awaken several hours later, her mind racked with questions about her future.

As she lay in the heavy silence with the darkness pressing in about her, she remembered Bart's advice. *"When counting sheep doesn't work—talk to the Shepherd."* And she did.

The children awoke to strange sounds coming from the bathroom as Trish's body retched with morning sickness. "I'll be okay in a minute, darlings," she told them as the three stood watching, concern written on each face. "Kerel, please go fix your sisters some cereal and milk. I'll be out as soon as I can. Don't worry. I'm fine."

"Mama, do you want me to get help for you? Maybe call Hildy? Or Mr. Ryan?"

"No!" she ordered in a weak voice. "Honest. I'm fine. Just give me a minute. Okay?"

As Trish applied a cool, damp washcloth to her face, she thanked the Lord she had the day off and didn't have to report to work at the Grayson House kitchen. Surely, she'd soon be through the morning sickness period of her pregnancy.

A rap sounded on the door late that afternoon and, after cautioning the girls to stand back, Trish opened it to find a leathery little man in overalls standing, hat in hand, with a toothless grin. "Mrs. Taylor? I'm Ben, the Kirkwoods' handyman. I have a note for you, and I'm supposed to wait for an answer."

Trish pushed open the screen and took the envelope from the man's hand. It was from Bart, inviting her and the children to attend church with his family the next morning. He explained he'd heard her parents were out of town, and he'd like to take both families to lunch after the morning service. Included were directions, the time of the service, and where they were to meet. She was to give a simple yes or no to Ben.

Church. How she'd missed attending since she'd left Wichita. Without a moment's thought, she pressed her hand against the screen door and smiled at the unlikely messenger. "Please tell Mr. Ryan the answer is yes."

He nodded, repeated the word, and backed off the porch with a half bow.

As he walked off toward the fence that separated the two properties, she called after him, "Thanks—Ben."

He waved and was gone.

The rest of the evening was spent taking baths, shining shoes, and pressing dresses. Once the girls had been tucked in for the night, Trish knelt beside the bed and once again thanked God for Bart Ryan.

❧

Bart and his three handsome sons, clothed in their Sunday best, their hair squeaky clean and slicked down, were waiting for Trish's family at the designated spot in the shopping mall's parking lot when the old station wagon chugged in and came to a stop beside Bart's large SUV.

Bart hurried to open their doors with a "Good morning, ladies." Then, one by one, as they exited the station wagon, he complimented them on how pretty each one looked, until he got to the driver. Taking her hand to assist her from the car, he leaned toward her and whispered privately in her ear, "Next to Charlotte, you're the prettiest pregnant woman I've ever seen!"

She was sure her cheeks were turning as rosy as the silk scarf about her neck. "You sure know how to treat a gal," she murmured.

Bart settled Zana into the car seat he said Andy had just outgrown, the other kids filled the back and third-row seats, and once everyone had buckled up, they headed for the church.

A friendly usher greeted Bart at the door of the vestibule with a warm handshake, then extended the same to Trish. It took the man a few minutes to find a pew with enough empty space to seat the group of eight, but eventually he did and they were seated with Bart and Trish in the center, the three girls beside her and his boys next to him.

Trish's heart soared as she joined Bart and the congregation in singing God's praise. She listened as Bart sang. He had a beautiful baritone voice and he sang with his all. It was obvious he was singing to his Lord. She found herself wondering why some Christian woman hadn't latched onto him years ago. Undoubtedly, in a congregation of this size, there were a number of eligible widows and single women. Although he introduced her to a number of women at the conclusion of the service, none of them seemed special to him, beyond friendship.

"Oh, Bart," Trish said as the eight of them walked to his SUV. "The people here are so friendly, and I love your pastor. He preaches the Word like our pastor in Wichita did. I felt right at home."

"Hey, good!" Zeb chimed in, with little Zana wrapped around his neck. "Why don't you come here all the time?"

"Yeah," Kyle agreed as he kicked a small rock across the parking lot, "this is a neat church."

"Kerel?" Bart queried as he put his arm around the adolescent's shoulder. "What do you think? Would you like to come to our church again? Maybe attend a Sunday school class and get acquainted with other girls your age?"

Trish was surprised to see her shy daughter lean into Bart's arm and even more surprised when she answered an eager yes without hesitation.

"So, Mama? What do you say? Can we entice you to come to church with us again?" Bart asked as he slid his hand beneath her elbow and guided her toward the SUV. "Next Sunday? Same time? Same place?"

Three girls and three boys and one handsome man waited for her answer.

She smiled at each one in turn. "A definite yes!"

The restaurant Bart's family had selected was only two blocks from the church and had an appetizing all-you-can-eat buffet. The hostess quickly located a table for eight and piled big platter-shaped plates in front of the group.

"You girls better stand back, 'cause when I hand these platters to my boys it gets dangerous. They take the shortest route to the mashed potatoes!" Bart warned.

"Yeah, Dad?" Zeb responded. "And who's always there first? You!" he added as he pointed his finger accusingly in his father's direction.

"Okay! Guilty as charged!" Bart confessed, still holding the pile of platters in his hands. "But what do we do before I pass these things out?"

"Pray!" Andy yelled, his voice loud enough for all those seated nearby to hear.

"You got it! Give that boy a silver dollar!" Bart quipped, not the least bit embarrassed by others knowing they intended to thank the Lord for their food before indulging. "Hold hands, gang. Let's make a prayer circle."

And there, standing around their table in front of all who would see them, Bart boldly prayed and thanked the Lord for the Word they'd heard in the morning service, for the food they were about to consume, and for giving the Ryan family the opportunity to lunch with the Taylor family. Trish greatly respected Bart Ryan. He seemed to be a man after God's own heart.

❧

By the time Mr. and Mrs. Grayson returned from their trip, Trish was well rested, encouraged, and ready for whatever verbal attack they might make on her. Her girls had settled into their new routine, and with the extra time she'd been able to spend at their little cabin she'd made it quite comfortable. It now seemed like home to the four of them.

Her parents were almost pleasant to her when she met them early Wednesday morning in the upstairs hallway, where she was stacking the clean bedding in the linen closet.

"Did you have a good trip?" she asked, truly interested, as they passed her.

Her father merely grunted, "Fine."

Her mother stopped long enough to smile and say, "Yes, thank you."

Trish straightened the contents of the linen closet shelves as she added the clean bedding and was nearly finished when the door to her mother's bedroom flew open. Olivia came gasping through the opening, her face white, her hands trembling.

By instinct, Trish ran to her mother, fearing she might be having a heart attack or had hurt herself in some way. "What is it, Mother?" she pleaded as she put her arm about Olivia's gaunt shoulders. Olivia pulled away from her and ran through the hallway screaming for Wilmer.

He rushed from his room at the sound of her voice. "What is it? Why are you so upset?"

"Someone has stolen my diamond ring and my emerald necklace! They're not in the safe!"

Wilmer rushed toward his wife as quickly as his weak legs could carry him, leaning heavily on his cane. "Are you sure? Could you have misplaced them?" he asked accusingly, which only upset her all the more.

"No! I didn't misplace them, Wilmer! You know how careful I am with my jewelry! I put it in the safe the minute I take it off!"

"Are you sure the safe was locked?" he queried, irritating her further.

Her eyes flashed with indignation. "Of course it was locked! How dare you suggest such a thing?"

"So? What are you saying, Olivia? That someone opened the safe and removed your jewelry?"

Olivia glared at her husband. "That, Wilmer," she said with a flip of her hand for emphasis, "is exactly what I am saying! I have been robbed!"

"Then call the police and the insurance company, Olivia," Wilmer ordered, throwing up his arms in disgust, apparently eager to let anyone else handle his wife and her problems. "That's why I pay those outlandish insurance premiums." With that, he turned and *tap-tapped* his way back to his room, leaning on his trusty cane.

Olivia spun around on her heels, her hands giving a twist of dismissal toward her husband, and glanced backward to her daughter. "You call the police. I'll call the insurance company!"

Trish moved quickly to the phone, ready to do her mother's bidding, and dialed 911.

The police arrived in record time. Olivia rambled on incoherently as the officer struggled in an attempt to learn what had happened. Finally, in desperation, he turned to Trish. "Young lady, did you see anyone lurking about the house or the grounds during the time the Graysons were gone?"

"No, sir. No one," she answered honestly.

"Other than the servants, was anyone else in the house while you were gone?" he asked Olivia, who was chattering away at the second officer.

"Yes. Our daughter, Margaret," Olivia responded between sentences.

"Is she home, ma'am? I'll need to talk to her," Detective Mercer asked as he entered Margaret's name on the report form on his clipboard.

"I'll get her," Trish volunteered, glad for a slight reprieve.

She returned shortly with Margaret following close behind.

"What's happened, Mother?" her sister questioned as she moved quickly to Olivia's side while giving the officers a startled look. "What're they doing here?"

Olivia smiled nervously at Margaret. "My diamond ring and my emerald necklace are missing from the safe," she murmured as her hand went to her throat. "Your father was furious! He—"

"But, Mother," Margaret countered, interrupting Olivia, "you always put your jewelry away when you take it off! Did someone break into the safe?"

"Please, ma'am," Detective Mercer asked in an official tone, "have you been home most of the time since your parents left town?"

Margaret nodded affirmatively. "Most of the time.

Although I was gone Sunday from about ten to two, when I drove into Denver for lunch."

"Have you noticed anyone lurking on or around the premises in the past few weeks? Especially over the weekend?"

Margaret shook her head. "No. No one. The servants and I were the only ones in the house." It seemed to Trish that her sister emphasized the word *servants,* knowing how Margaret felt about her returning home.

The detective appeared to notice and asked, "Do you have someone in mind, Miss Grayson? Perhaps a newly hired employee or a former employee who might have been disgruntled?"

Margaret glanced about awkwardly, then responded in a vague, noncommittal way as she cast a quick glance toward her sister. "Not really. . .only—"

"Only what, Miss Grayson?" he asked as if determined to pry an answer from her.

Olivia moved to Trish's side. "This young woman came to work for us recently, but. . ." Her voice wavered as she searched for words. "She comes from a good family. We've known her for years. I'm sure she's trustworthy, as are our other servants." Then, addressing her daughter as an employee, she ordered, "You may go now. I'm sure Hildy needs you in the kitchen."

Although Trish was hurt by her mother's deception, she was glad for a chance to remove herself from the tense situation regarding the theft.

"What're they doin' now?" Hildy stared at Trish as she entered the kitchen. "I suppose we're all suspects, seein' we were the only ones in the house while your parents were gone."

Trish plopped onto the stool at the end of the counter and absentmindedly began rearranging the apples waiting to be peeled for a pie. "She gave the detective the impression I was recently hired, never a hint that I was her daughter. But she vouched for all of us servants equally."

Hildy eyed the woman she'd known since babyhood with a look of both surprise and compassion. "I'm so sorry, honey."

Trish folded her hands in her lap, her eyes downcast. "I never meant to hurt them. Honest, I didn't. But I couldn't kill my own baby. Not even if it meant defying my parents. Can you understand that?"

The older woman crossed the kitchen floor and placed her big arm about Trish's shoulders. "Of course, Hildy understands. I've never told anyone around here, but I guess I can tell you. I made that same decision when I was your age. I kept my baby, too. Only difference was, my boyfriend didn't stand by me like Jake stood by you. I had to make it on my own. That's why I became a cook. It was the only job I could get with no more education than I had. I couldn't say anything at the time, but I was real proud of you, Trish. Keepin' that baby like you did."

Trish reached up and patted the rounded hand that rested on her shoulder. "Hildy, thanks. Your support means a lot to me." As she lifted her eyes to her friend, she knew she could confide in Hildy, that she would never betray her. "Hildy. . ."

"What, honey? What is it? You can tell Hildy."

"I'm. . .pregnant."

The older woman backed off with a gasp as her hand moved to cover her mouth. "Pregnant? But—"

"The baby is Jake's, Hildy. My dead husband's child!"

"Oh, honey. When're you due? Do your folks know?"

Trish shook her head. "No, and I can't imagine what they'll do when they find out. The children and I may be out on the street. I'm nine or ten weeks along, but—"

Hildy placed her hand on Trish's. "We'll just have to keep it a secret as long as we can. What can I do to help?"

Trish smiled at Hildy. "You've already helped by letting me tell you. But, please, if anyone asks anything about me, you must tell the truth. I won't have you, or anyone else, lying for me."

ﻬ

"Hey, Bart. Telephone!" Ruth Flint called loudly as she waved her arms furiously at the man driving the hi-loader.

The drone of the heavy engine stopped and it suddenly became quiet in the nursery's yard as Bart crawled down from his seat, wiping sweat from his brow with a red bandanna. "Who is it?"

The woman handed him the cordless phone. "Don't know."

"Bart Ryan," he said into the receiver.

"Bart? It's me."

His chin lifted. "Trish? What's wrong? You sound troubled."

"I shouldn't have called you. It's just—well, I needed you—"

He moved quickly into the potting shed, seeking privacy. "Trish! Do you want me to come there? What's wrong?"

"Some of my mother's jewelry was stolen. The police were here. It was awful. I just wanted to hear your voice, Bart. You've become my rock. I—shouldn't have bothered you. I'm sorry. I'll talk to you later."

He grasped the phone with both hands, as if to keep her on the line. "No, Trish," he ordered. "Don't hang up! I'm here for you. Now, and anytime!"

"There's nothing you can do, Bart. I guess my pregnancy is making my hormones go crazy. I'm a big girl. I should be able to handle this myself. It's just—"

"It's just that you've been through way more than your share of trouble lately. You're handling it better than most women I know could. I'm coming—"

"No!" she said emphatically. "I have to finish out my day and you're busy. Besides, I don't want to get you involved. If my parents knew you even knew me—"

"I don't care, Trish. I'm proud to be your friend."

"But," she said with great concern, "my parents are not known for their compassion, especially in business. I don't want to be the cause—"

"Forget that, Trish. You are not the cause of anything. I became your friend because I wanted to. You never held anything back. You were perfectly honest with me right from the beginning. I walked into this relationship of ours with my eyes wide open. I know what the consequences might be if they find out. I lived without their business before, I can do it again."

"Thanks, Bart. It helps me to hear you say that. But please, let's not take any chances on them finding out, okay? No need to invite trouble. I just needed to hear your voice. But remember, if we are found out we must be honest."

"I told you I've never condoned lying. Meet me tonight— at our place. I'll bring the boys and we'll pick up a picnic supper for eight. Six o'clock, okay?"

"Oh, yes," she responded, delight evident in her voice. "Six will be fine for us. Are you sure it's not too early for you?"

"Six it is. And, Trish—chin up! Okay?"

❧

Bart leaned against the back of the moldy wooden bench in the dilapidated gazebo and locked his hands behind his head, the laughter of children at play filling his ears and thoughts of Trish filling his mind. He admired her spunk, both now, and all those years ago.

He felt a light touch on his shoulder. "Bart?"

He straightened and turned quickly to find the subject of his thoughts standing behind him, leaning over the railing and wearing a big smile on her pretty face.

"Where were you?" she asked coyly as she gave his arm a quick pinch. "You were so deep in thought, I was almost afraid to disturb you!"

His hand covered hers as he looked into her big, round, inquisitive eyes. "I was deep in thought," he answered apologetically. "I was thinking about—you."

"Me?"

He pursed his lips. "Uh-huh. You. And about all the crazy things you're going through. I care about you—and the girls—and that baby you're carrying."

"Guess that's the reason I turn to you so often. You're about the only person around here who does care," she stated with a strained laugh as she circled the gazebo and dropped down beside him. "Actually—you're it! The only person, except Hildy, that is."

"Hildy?" he asked, his brows raised in surprise. "The cook?"

Trish uttered a slight chuckle. "Uh-huh. I told her I was pregnant."

Bart frowned. "Was that was a good idea? Think you can trust her to keep your secret?"

She nodded. "I know I can trust her, Bart. Outside of you, she's probably the only one I can trust. But I did tell her I didn't want her to lie for me."

"So. Tell me all about what happened today."

Trish looked from the huge white sacks on the picnic table to her friend. "After supper. Okay? That'll be soon enough. I feel better already, just being here with you—and the boys."

"Dad," Zeb pleaded as he tossed a baseball toward his father, "when we gonna eat? I'm hungry!"

"Now!" his father answered as he caught the ball and hurled it back. "Soup's on, everyone! Grab hands and let's pray! Would you like the honor, Zeb?"

After Zeb eloquently thanked the Lord for the food, the two families gathered around the rickety old table. Zeb and Kerel set out paper plates and utensils while Bart and Trish passed out the cartons of potato salad, coleslaw, mashed potatoes and gravy, biscuits, and crunchy fried chicken to the eager takers.

Once the food was devoured and the mess cleaned up, the two adults seated themselves on the gazebo's bench and watched as their children skipped rocks across the stream.

"Your boys are wonderful, Bart. You've done a good job with them." Trish smoothed her skirt, flaring it out across the bench as she spoke.

"Hey, I was about to say the same thing about you and your girls! You beat me to it. No fair!" He playfully gave her a jab with his elbow. "Now, tell me!"

Trish drew a deep breath and told him the whole story.

"She referred to you as a new hire? That's incredible!"

"I didn't know what to say. I didn't expect her to brag about the prodigal daughter returning home, but. . ." She lowered her gaze. "It hurt, Bart."

His fingers quickly found and gripped hers. "I know," he consoled sympathetically. "It'd hurt me if my mom ever did that to me. You had every right to be upset."

She lifted questioning eyes to his. "What's she going to do when she learns I'm pregnant? Again?"

"Maybe she'll respond differently this time. Maybe even welcome a new grandchild."

Trish's brows knitted into justified concern. "Like she welcomed the three grandchildren I brought with me? I don't think so. Neither she nor my father is the least bit concerned about having grandchildren. Let's not kid ourselves."

"So? When are you going to tell them about the baby you're carrying?" he asked cautiously.

Trish pulled from his grasp and stood to her feet. "I don't know. Not any sooner than I have to, I guess," she said with reluctance. "I can't cover it forever."

"And you shouldn't have to, Trish. This should be a happy time in your life. To think that you are carrying one of God's creations—well, you ought to be able to shout it from the housetops instead of having to hide its existence."

"I know. God has been so good to me." She turned toward her children who were clapping and cheering for Bart's boys as they skipped the rocks over the water's surface. "I look at my three beautiful, healthy daughters and I have to praise Him. To think that He would trust me to raise them for Him—well, the whole idea is overwhelming! Now, for some reason known only to Him, He's giving me another baby to raise. He must think I have some worth!"

Bart jumped to his feet. "Trish! How can you doubt your value as a mother? As a human being? Of course God trusts you. Look at those girls, Trish! No one could've done a better job than you have. You can't let your mother's attitude cast doubt on your capabilities. That's her problem, not yours! She's the one who's missing out on the good things of life. It's you who should feel sorry for her. You have the things that really count in life. Things money can't buy. She has only material possessions."

"Like her precious jewelry?"

"Exactly," he reiterated with a slap to his knee. "Things that can be easily replaced. Baubles, bangles, and things are only outward symbols of wealth to impress others. Remember what the Scripture says: 'What good will it be for a man if he gains the whole world, yet forfeits his soul?' Your mother may have wealth, Trish. But you have God. And He cares about you. Don't ever forget it!"

"But I'm afraid she suspects I took her jewelry, even though she vouched for me—she's probably afraid of another scandal. I had the time, and in her eyes, I had the motive. I'm broke!"

"You'll just have to trust God to work this out. And," he said with a sly grin, "don't you worry about being cast out onto the street. I'd never let that happen to you. If they ever turn you out, you come to me. You hear? I mean it, Trish. I'm here for you!"

She placed her hand in his. "Thanks, Bart. I hope that never happens, but if it does, I promise I'll come to you. I'd need your wise counsel."

He pulled her to him and encircled her trembling body

with his embrace, hoping to give her the comfort she needed so badly after her mother's searing rejection. "And I do care, Trish. I'm very concerned about you."

"I know," she whispered softly.

With the fingers of one hand, he lifted her chin and raised her face to his. "You're a beautiful woman, Trish. Jake was one lucky man to have you as his wife."

A sudden scream seized their attention as Kerel called out loudly from the edge of the little stream, where the group of children were kneeling around her little sister. "Mom, Zana cut her leg on a rock! It's bleeding!"

Bart grabbed Trish by the hand and the two rushed to the tiny girl, who'd stumbled and fallen against a sharp rock protruding through the otherwise grassy water's edge.

"Now, honey," he told Zana as he held her on his lap and wrapped his pristine white hanky around her tiny knee, "it's not as bad as it looks. Just scratched up the surface a bit. You'll be good as new in a day or two."

Zana quieted down at the soothing sound of his voice and soon seemed to almost forget about her mishap.

"I'll carry you as far as I can, but you'll have to walk the rest of the way. You're too heavy for your mother to carry you in her. . ." He winked at the expectant mother. "You're getting to be a big girl now. Can you promise Uncle Bart you'll walk like a big girl, so Mommy won't have to carry you?"

Little Zana nodded as Bart dried her eyes with a paper napkin left over from their picnic.

He gathered her up in his arms, instructed his sons to wait for him by the gazebo, and carried her to the clearing before setting her on her feet. "Wish I could carry you all the way, honey, but I can't. Now hold Mommy's hand and you girls be careful crossing the meadow."

The young mother took her small daughter's hand with an air of pride. "Don't you think you should thank Bart, Zana?

For carrying you?"

He put up a hand of protest. "No thanks needed, Zana. The pleasure was all mine. Not often an old guy like me gets to enjoy the company of four such beautiful women."

"Thanks, Bart. You don't know what your friendship means to us. I'm afraid, at times, I take advantage of it. Seems I'm always burdening you with my troubles."

He stepped forward and rested a reassuring hand on her shoulder. "You have given me nothing I haven't asked for. I want you to come to me, Trish. I've told you that before, and I meant it. Anytime."

She cupped her hand over his and smiled up into his face. "Remember that when I call you in the middle of the night!"

"Phone's right by the bed. It'd be no trouble at all. Now you girls better get a move on. It'll be dark soon."

six

As chairman of the hospital benefit ball, Olivia spent most of her time on the phone or in planning meetings away from Grayson House, making Trish's life much easier to manage. Her father and his attorney were tied up most days in acquisition meetings. Other than an occasional visit from Detective Mercer, very few visitors called.

In her free time, Trish busied herself making new curtains for the girls' bedroom with fabric Hildy had given her. She and the children worked in the yard around the little cabin and soon had the lawn weed free. She'd even planted several small flowering bushes, courtesy of Ryan Garden and Landscape. With their hard work, the cabin soon looked like a real home. She wished she could invite Bart and the boys to come and see what they'd done, but she knew that was impossible, although he'd said he was willing to take that chance.

The weeks passed quickly. School would soon be starting, and Trish had no idea what she was going to do with Zana. She'd saved every bit of her meager salary, knowing she might have to pay a babysitter. Each night, she prayed and asked the Lord to provide for Zana's care.

Her mother's stolen jewelry had been all but forgotten by everyone but the insurance company that had replaced the valuable pieces. Detective Mercer had stopped coming by.

"Trish, come in here," Olivia ordered as her daughter entered the kitchen one morning in late August. "I've been wondering what you are planning to do with that youngest daughter of yours when school starts."

Trish stared at Olivia in surprise and stammered, "I—ah—

I'm not sure. Put her at a babysitter's perhaps. Maybe I can find a government-subsidized program. Why do you ask?"

Olivia appeared frustrated with the answer and spoke firmly. "I happen to be on the Community Improvement Board. It wouldn't do to have someone find out that a member of the Grayson household is receiving government help!"

"But—"

"That is not an option, Patricia. I have a solution. I'll have Martin stock your old bedroom with toys appropriate for a girl her age, along with a VCR and a number of videos, maybe a couple dozen books—you know, things that will keep her occupied during the day while you work here in the house. That way, you'll be able to keep an eye on her."

Trish was so moved by her mother's solution, she reached out to touch her arm, but Olivia pulled away. Once again assuming the position of a servant, Trish said, "Thank you. That relieves my mind. I wasn't sure what I was going to do—"

"Just be sure she stays in that room or with Hildy."

Trish's joy at being able to keep little Zana close to her overshadowed any hurt she might have felt from her mother's coolness. One of her problems had been solved.

"Are you putting on a little weight, Patricia?" her mother asked as she eyed her. "You seem—fuller than when you arrived."

Trish held her breath and tried to pull her stomach in without being too obvious. "Yes, a few pounds. Perhaps I need to start walking regularly—instead of enjoying Hildy's cooking." She hoped her mother would accept her feeble explanation.

Apparently, Olivia either accepted her answer or simply was not concerned. Either way, she left Trish standing in the hall and entered her bedroom, closing the door behind her.

Trish turned at the sound of footsteps and the *tap, tap* of her father's cane as he moved down the hallway toward her. "Good morning, Father."

Mr. Grayson stopped directly before her and stood staring at his daughter. "You know, Patricia, if you'd listened to me and stayed away from that Jake Taylor, you'd probably be married to a man who could give you the kind of life your mother and I had envisioned for you. You'd be playing tennis at the country club right now instead of vacuuming and working as a maid. But, no! You had to defy me and your mother, and run off with that boy! I get so mad when I think—"

She stepped back, offended by his unprovoked verbal attack. "Please, Father. That happened thirteen years ago. Are you going to carry this vendetta against me for the rest of your life?"

"Me?" the old man clamored with a thump of his cane on the floor. "It was you who made us the laughingstock of this community. We warned you. You should never have had that baby! It would've been so simple to get rid of it. But no! You were so noble and sanctimonious you wanted to have that baby—even if it embarrassed your family. You were a spiteful, headstrong teenager with no regard for us." He pointed the tip of his cane toward the stairway. "If it wasn't for your mother, you'd never have been allowed to come back to Grayson House."

Trish stepped to one side and allowed her father to pass, knowing his heart was so hardened there was only one person could speak to him and heal him. God!

❧

Bart clicked the shutdown feature on his computer and watched as the screen went black and the hum of the hard drive ceased, the figures he'd entered still etched in his memory.

Visions of Trish and the children filled his mind. It was hard for him to imagine soft-spoken, sweet-natured Trish standing up to her crusty old father and her outspoken mother.

She had so few options in her life. Surely her parents wouldn't turn her out when they found out about her pregnancy, would they? And, if they did, how would she make it? He'd said he would never allow her to be turned out onto the street, that she could always come to him, hadn't he?

Bart leaned back in his desk chair and locked his hands behind his head, his eyes closed in deep, searching thought. Although he'd meant what he'd said, at the time he hadn't thoroughly considered the ramifications of such a decision. A few weeks ago, he'd never even heard her name, didn't know she existed. Who was he to make such an offer to a near stranger? Actually, worse than a near stranger. She was the disinherited daughter of his business's largest client! A decision like that could really make an impact on his financial status. Bart had committed to several long-term leases on new equipment that could become a burden without the Grayson account.

Yet hadn't God commanded in His Word that we should care for widows and orphans? As a Christian man and a deacon in his church, could he turn his back on Trish—a widow with three children and one on the way—and do it with a clear conscience?

Bart fell to his knees beside his desk and prayed. Prayed for God's leading in his new friend's life. Prayed God would supply her needs. Prayed for her children and the baby she was carrying. And most of all, prayed that if God saw fit to use him in Trish's life, the Lord would make him willing to do whatever was necessary to help her.

❧

The moonlight shining through the window of the little caretaker's cabin illuminated Trish's room with a silvery glow. She'd lain awake for hours, wondering what would be the best way to tell her parents about her pregnancy—and how they would react. Finally, following Bart's advice, she talked to the

Shepherd and turned it over to Him. Sleep came almost immediately.

Without warning, a sharp, stabbing pain split through her abdomen, bringing her knees to her chest as she clenched her fists in agony. She moaned, but pressed her lips between her teeth to keep from crying out and waking her children. As soon as the pain subsided, she rushed into the bathroom and arched her body over the tiny, rust-stained sink, trying to steady herself as her hands grasped its edges in panic. It was then she saw them. Spots of blood on her gown!

She'd never had a miscarriage. Was this the way one started? Was this the Lord's way of solving her problem?

A tiny hand tugged on her gown. "Mama, are you sick again?" little Zana asked as she rubbed her sleepy eyes and yawned.

Trish took a deep breath and clutched the area on her gown where the crimson red stains were. "Mama's okay. Go back to bed, Honey. Mama will be there soon. Okay?"

She watched as the little girl padded across the bedroom floor and climbed beneath the covers before closing the bathroom door, fearing the worst as the spotting continued.

Oh, God, she prayed from the depths of her broken heart, *I don't know what to do. I'm so alone. If this is Your will, let me have a miscarriage.*

An eternity later, the rosy glow of daylight found the frightened mother curled up beside her daughter, watching the clock, waiting for the clinic to open so she could call Dr. Brewer.

All sorts of things tumbled through her mind. Losing the baby now would be the easiest solution to her problems. The doctor, Bart, and Hildy were the only ones who knew she was pregnant. No one else would ever have to know.

But God had seen fit to give her this fourth child, this child of Jake's. And, despite all the trouble its arrival would cause and all the financial hardships she would face, she wanted it! For the first time since she'd discovered she was pregnant, she knew giving birth to this child was every bit as important to her as the birth of Kerel, her firstborn, and her prayer changed.

God, my life is in Your hands. I want Your will to be done. And I want this baby if it is in Your will. I'm Yours, Lord. Do with me as You see fit. I know You'll take care of me and my little family. Make me a living testimony for You. And make me strong, Lord. Make me strong!

"You must come in as soon as possible, Mrs. Taylor," Dr. Brewer directed with firmness. "This may not be cause for alarm but we can't take any chances. Try to get someone to drive you. We don't want you fainting and having an accident on the way."

"Is that necessary, Dr. Brewer?" Trish asked quickly. "I really don—"

"Yes," Dr. Brewer replied firmly, "you shouldn't come alone."

Trish hung up the phone slowly. There was no one to drive her into Denver. Except. . .

No, she couldn't call him.

But who?

Who else could she turn to, except Bart?

&

Bart Ryan picked up the phone in his office at Ryan Garden and Landscape with his free hand, his coffee mug in the other. "Ryan, here."

At first, no one responded, then an almost inaudible, "Bart?"

He stiffened. "Trish?"

"Yes. It's me. But I shouldn't have called you. I'm sorry. Good—"

"Wait!" he shouted into the phone. "Don't hang up, Trish. What's the matter?" The silence hung thick as he waited for her reply. "Trish?"

"I'm—spotting."

He straightened in his chair, the coffee cup coming down with a plunk on the desk. He'd heard those very words, seventeen years ago—when Charlotte was expecting Zeb. "When did it start?"

"About four this morning."

"Have you called the doctor?"

"Yes. She wants me to come in as soon as I can."

He glanced at his watch. "I'll be there in fifteen minutes. Be ready." It was a decision made without hesitation.

"I can't ask you to—"

"You didn't ask me. I volunteered. Now hang up the phone. I'll come in my truck so no one will question why I'm on the grounds of Grayson House. What about the girls?"

"Hildy is going to check on them every hour. They'll be fine." She took a deep breath. "Ar—are you sure you want to do this?"

He grinned into the phone. "Sure I want to do it. See you in fifteen!"

He glanced heavenward as he reached for his ball cap. "Wow, Lord! You sure didn't waste any time putting my vows to the test."

☙

The Ryan Garden and Landscape truck pulled into the empty space at the curb in front of Denver's free clinic and came to a stop. "Wait. Let me get the door," Bart commanded as he leaped out the driver's side and bounded around the truck.

Trish sat still, her hands splayed across her abdomen. "Thank you," she said sincerely as she accepted his hand and exited the vehicle. "I'll be back as soon—"

"I'm going in with you." Sliding his hand under her elbow, he guided her toward the clinic's door.

"But, Bart!" she protested as she pulled from his grasp.

"No buts about it. I'm going."

"I'm Patricia Taylor. Dr. Brewer wanted me to come in," Trish told the receptionist.

Bart stood by her side.

"She's expecting you," the woman answered matter-of-factly. "Go right in."

"I'll wait out here." He headed for a nearby empty chair.

❧

"You should be fine with a few days' bed rest," Dr. Brewer told her fifteen minutes later as she disposed of the rubber gloves. "And try to stay calm. Stress is the last thing you need right now."

Trish's brows rose. "Stress? That would cause the spotting?"

"Any physical difficulties can magnify themselves when you're stressed. If you have any more problems or the spotting continues, call me. Okay?"

"Sure. Okay," Trish replied quietly. "It's just that I don't know how I'm going to manage bed rest. I have to work."

"Surely your boss will let you off—under the circumstances," Dr. Brewer said with a tilt of her head.

"I'll manage somehow, and thanks for everything."

Bart jumped to his feet when the door to the waiting room opened. "You okay?" He rushed to Trish's side and wrapped her hand in his.

She looked around warily. "I'll tell you when we get outside."

The two made their way to the truck with Bart hovering over her like a doting grandma.

"I'm going to be fine, Bart. So is the baby," she told him as he assisted her into the pickup. "I just need to avoid stress."

"Is that all she said?" he asked before closing her door. "Can you take a few pills?"

She managed a weak smile. "Not exactly."

He slammed the door and hurried around to the driver's side, then crawled in quickly beside her. "Then what exactly?"

"Something I can't manage."

"Like what?"

She fidgeted a bit and replied softly. "Bed rest."

"Bed rest? Then you have to do it, Trish," he told her compassionately as he squeezed her hand. "You don't want to lose that baby, do you?"

Her eyes searched his. "Yesterday, I might have said yes. But, early this morning, when I thought I might actually lose my baby, I suddenly realized I wanted it! I prayed and told the Lord I was willing to do whatever it takes." Her hand gripped his tightly. "I very much want this baby!"

❧

Upon her return home, Hildy welcomed her with good news. Her mother was going to New York City for a few days with some of her friends to do some shopping.

Thanks to her mother's impromptu trip, Trish was able to spend the next four days in bed. Surprisingly, her girls hadn't questioned their mother's unusual behavior, assuming she had the flu, but she'd have to tell them about the baby soon.

On the fourth day of her confinement, Bart showed up at the door with a huge bouquet of fresh cut flowers.

"Did anyone see you come here?" she questioned with great concern for her friend.

"Nope—parked over at the Kirkwoods' and walked in through the meadow. With Mrs. Grayson out of town, I figured it'd be safe to drive right up to your door, but I knew that'd worry you, and I didn't want to cause any of that stress the doc told you to avoid." He gave her a winsome smile as he pulled a chair up beside the bed.

A frown creased her forehead as she accepted his flowers and held them to her breast. "Oh, Bart, I'm so glad to see you, but please don't put yourself in jeopardy."

His face took on a somber look. "What do you think they'll do? When they find out?"

"Remember, this is Jake's baby. I'm sure they'll react the

same way they did the first time. That is, if they believe it is Jake's baby. My dear father has already questioned the paternity of my two younger children."

"You're kidding! When?"

"When I arrived. That very first day."

"Aw, Trish." His voice was kind and sympathetic. "How could he? You're his daughter. Surely he didn't mean it the way it sounded."

Trish's fingers went to her temples. "Oh, but he did. He made me feel like a cheap—"

Bart's finger tapped her lips to silence her. "Don't, Trish! Don't say it! You're a fine woman. That man needs help."

A small rush of air escaped from her lungs. "Don't let *him* hear you say that!"

"I'm praying for him—and your mother, Trish. They need the Lord in a big way!"

"I know. I'm praying for them, too. And I have forgiven them. Honest, I have. Long ago."

He grinned. "Why doesn't that surprise me?"

She glanced at the clock on the nightstand. "I know you have better things to do with your time than sit here with me. Thank you for coming, and for the flowers." She ducked her head shyly. "I've been wishing I could see you."

"Really? You have?"

"Yes. Seeing you, and being with you and the boys—well, you're the best thing that's happened to me in a long time."

He took her hand in his and stroked it with his long, lean fingers. "I wish there was some way I could spare you all of this."

"But there isn't."

His face brightened. "I could marry you—tell your folks this baby is mine!"

seven

She gasped. "Don't kid like that. We don't want any rumors to get started!"

With an infectious smile, he went on, "I think it's a good idea. The boys and I need a woman in the house. And from the looks of my boys when they're with your girls, they'd love to have a bunch of sisters to tease!"

She snickered. His presence always put her in a good mood. "We'd be quite a family, all right! They'd send you to the loony bin, taking on a group like mine. But thanks for the offer. I needed a good laugh! Just be glad you weren't speaking into an audio recorder. I might have tried to hold you to it when my folks toss me and my girls out on our ears!"

"Don't laugh too hard, little lady!" he said, his tone serious once again. "If that's what it takes to keep a roof over your head and food on your table, I'd do it!"

She reached out and touched his broad shoulder. "You know, I believe you would."

                          *

By the time Olivia returned from her trip, Trish was back to work and her physical condition had improved.

"Did you have a good time in New York City?" Trish asked her mother as she was dusting her bedroom.

"Yes, I did," Olivia answered as she gave her daughter an uninterested look. "By the way, your father and I are entertaining a few close friends this Saturday night. I'd prefer that you and the children stay away from Grayson House. It would be a shame for anyone to recognize you and bring up all those old memories and accusations."

Trish bit her lip. "Yes, Mother."

"See that you do what your mother says," Wilmer added as he joined his wife. "You've caused enough problems, turning up on our doorstep with your brood of children like you did. I don't want to have to explain your present predicament to our friends. Do us the courtesy of staying out of sight for the evening."

He couldn't have hurt her more if he'd stabbed her through the heart with a dagger, but she'd never let him know and stood there quietly, taking it. "Yes, Father."

"See that you do, Patricia." With that, he turned and tapped his way on down the hall to his bedroom, with Olivia at his side.

Trish rubbed her hand across her rounding abdomen. Soon everyone would know about her baby. The time had come to separate herself from Bart. No matter how painful that separation would be. She'd write him a note, that way she wouldn't have to see his face when she told him.

❧

Bart recognized the handwriting immediately when he sorted through the morning mail. It was Trish's. The little note was simple:

Dear Bart,

I'm so afraid someone is going to find out how much you've helped me and my family. I couldn't bear it if you, or your business, suffered because of me. You are the best friend I've ever had. I love you and your boys, and I will be praying for you. Please stay away from me. It's best for all of us.

Your friend for life,
Trish

Bart held the note in his hand and read it again. Mixed emotions of love, anger, indignation, and contempt flowed through him, causing his blood pressure to rise to the boiling point. Had something happened at Grayson House to bring this on? He had to find out. No way was he going to let Trish bow out of his life this easily. Others may abandon her, but he would not.

❧

Trish sat in the living room of the little caretaker's cabin with a bag of calico patches in her lap, her two older daughters prone on the worn rug, playing a game of checkers while Zana played with her doll. Hildy had given her the quilt she'd started many years ago, along with several bags of ready-cut patches, in hopes it would take the expectant mother's mind off her condition.

One by one, she pinned and pieced the patches, watching the quilt grow beneath her fingertips as she worked steadily. She found the constant rhythm of the needle and thread to be cathartic.

A light rap on the window startled her, and she turned to see Bart's concerned face peering in through the glass. She quickly moved to open the door and step out onto the porch. "What are you doing here? Didn't you get my note? Did anyone see you?"

"No one saw me," he whispered. "I was careful. Yes, I got your note. That's why I waited until after dark. I didn't want to cause you any trouble."

Her hand closed over his wrist. "It's you I'm worried about. Oh, Bart. You know how spiteful my parents can be. Please, you must go. Now!" She tried to steer him toward the steps of the little porch, but he wouldn't budge.

"Trish! I'm not a coward. I refuse to let your folks' reputation intimidate me. In fact, I'm tempted to go up to the main house right now and tell them what I think of their uppity ways."

Trish placed her finger across his lips and cautioned, "Shh! Someone might hear you!"

He grabbed her hand in his and pressed it to his lips. "For you, I'll be quiet. I don't want them taking my actions out on you. But, Trish! If your father were a few years younger and in better health—I'd go up there and bust him in the nose!"

"You—a Christian man? Somehow I can't see that happening!"

"I'm sorry, Trish. But that's exactly what I'd like to do. His attitude toward you brings out the worst in me!" His fist rammed the palm of his other hand for emphasis. "I can't stand to see them hurt you this way!" His hand sought hers in the semidarkness.

His touch was warm, soothing, but the cool night air engulfed her and she shivered.

"You're cold," he whispered as he drew her to him and wrapped her in the warmth of his embrace.

She snuggled in close to his body, basking in the safety and security she felt there. "I'm fine—now."

She stood there, knowing this had to be the last time they'd be together like this.

With the tip of his finger, Bart lifted her chin and raised her face to his. "Please, Trish. Don't let things end this way. I'm willing to take a chance. If we continue to be discreet, maybe they won't find out we're seeing one another."

With both palms pressing against his chest, Trish pushed away, creating a distance between them as she shook her head. "Bart, you and the boys have added so much to our lives, but I can't have them, or you, lying for me."

"We're not! No one has ever asked us about you. Other than the people at church, no one has any idea we're seeing one another. I'd never ask my boys to lie. I've never even told them to keep our relationship a secret!"

"Don't you see? I can't take any chances. I have to follow my parents' instructions to the letter. I have three little girls who are depending on me." She smiled and patted her abdomen. "And this little one, too. Oh, oh!"

"What? What is it, Trish?"

"Nothing to be concerned about," she said, patting her belly. "The baby just gave a good kick, that's all!" Her palm rotated soothingly across her abdomen.

Bart gave her a sheepish grin. "May I?"

"May you?" she asked with a slight frown, unsure what he was asking. "May you what?"

"Feel it kick?" He stepped back as though embarrassed. "I know that's asking a lot, Trish. But I remember the wonderful experience of feeling my boys kick when Charlotte was pregnant. It was like touching a miracle. I have no right. I'm sorry, I shouldn't have asked." He lowered his head apologetically.

"No right? Who came to my rescue and took me to the doctor when I was spotting? Whose encouragement cheered me when I was so down I couldn't look up? You, Bart."

She reached for his hand and carefully placed it at her swollen waistline. "Show Bart how you can kick, little baby!"

As if on cue, the baby within her gave a mighty kick against Bart's warm hand.

"He did it! Oh, Trish! I felt him kick!"

Trish laughed aloud. "He? You think it's a he? That just may be a little girl kicking at you, Mr. Ryan!"

"Naw," he said with a grin that exploded across his face in the shadows of the porch. "You're talking to a pro. I've had three boys, remember? I know how they kick, and that was definitely a male kick! A football player's kick! Mark my words, lady. That baby is a boy!"

"I say it's another girl." Trish giggled like a schoolgirl. "That's exactly the way my girls kicked! I'd say my daughters are going to have another little sister. With all the girls' things I have boxed away, a girl would be nice. I wouldn't have to buy a thing, except diapers. I sure don't have the money for new baby clothes!"

The baby kicked again. This time harder than the last.

"Nope!" he retorted. "That baby is a boy. No girl could kick like that. I'm so sure of it, I'll make a deal with you. If this baby is a boy, like I say he is, I'll buy all the clothes the kid will need for the first year of his life. And I'll throw in some of my boys' hand-me-downs! How's that for a deal?"

She lifted his hand from her abdomen and gave it a squeeze. "What if she's a girl? Will you eat crow?" she asked as a grin curled her lips. Her spirits always seemed to soar when this man was around.

"Crow? Umm, maybe not. But I'll treat you and the girls to more fried chicken! Will that do?"

Her demeanor grew serious. "Bart, I love seeing you, being with you. But this has got to stop. This has to be our last time together!"

He cupped her chin in his hand and gazed into her eyes. "I'm not sure that's possible, Trish. You've become an important part of my life. Much more than a friend. And who would drive you to the doctor if I wasn't around?"

"I'll drive myself."

"To Denver? In that station wagon? No, you can't do that, Trish."

"Somehow I'll work it out. I can't continue to depend on you, Bart." She turned away from him. "We—"

"Trish, no. Don't send me away."

"I have to. Good-bye, Bart. And thank you for everything. I'll never be able to repay you—"

"I don't want repayment, Trish! I want—"

"No, we have to end this now. Please, go. Don't make this any harder than it is. Just go. Please!"

Bart grabbed her by the shoulders and spun her around to face him. "Trish, I . . ."

Without warning, she felt his arms encircling her, his lips pressing on hers, and she couldn't pull away. She didn't want to pull away.

When the kiss ended, he released her and backed down the steps, any expression on his face masked by the darkness of the night. "Sorry. I don't know what came over me, but I had to do that," he said softly. "I'll go, if that's what you want."

"It's what we have to do," she murmured regretfully.

"Trish. I'm here for you. Anytime you need me, just call. Promise?"

"I promise. And, Bart. Thank you."

As he disappeared into the thick shadows of the night, she touched her fingertips to her lips and remembered the kiss.

છે

Bart stood in the grove just beyond the shed and watched as the door closed behind Trish. *Whatever possessed me? I just kissed a pregnant woman!* He shook his head, trying to clear it. He suddenly realized he'd wanted to kiss her since the time he'd overheard her at the gazebo, crying out to God about her pregnancy.

Things had changed radically since the Taylor family had entered his life. Trish and her children were constantly on his mind. He'd begun planning his days and evenings around them. So had his boys. They bugged him constantly to see the girls.

Although he was willing to put his business on the line to see her, he realized she had much more at stake. He had his business to fall back on, a business that provided his family's needs more than adequately. She had nothing. He vowed, somehow, he would help her, with or without her consent. *Lord, guide me. Show me how to help this family—without hurting them.*

છે

"Patricia, my bathtub has spots on it," Margaret complained when her sister brought clean towels for her bathroom the next morning. "I will not tolerate spots, do you hear?"

Trish wanted to defend herself. It was Anna who had cleaned her sister's bathroom, not her. But, not wanting to have Margaret's wrath fall on her friend and coworker, she said nothing.

Her mother was waiting in the hall with a strange expression on her face. "Patricia. Come here. I want to talk to you."

She shifted the remaining towels in front of her and sucked in her stomach. "Yes, Mother?"

"Have you seen my heart-shaped diamond brooch? I may have left it on my dresser last night, after your father and I returned from the theater."

Trish frowned. "No, Mother. I haven't been in your room this morning."

Olivia looked thoughtful. "Maybe I put it in the safe."

Trish followed her mother into the bedroom and on into the bath, the clean towels in her arms.

"It's not here!" Olivia yelled, her voice high-pitched as she checked through the safe's contents. "Oh, Wilmer will have a fit! What is happening to my jewelry?"

"I don't know, Mother," Trish answered with concern as she moved back into the bedroom. "Have you heard any more from Detective Mercer? Did they ever recover your other pieces?"

"No! Nothing! As far as I know, they're still missing. Of course, the insurance company replaced the stolen pieces, but surely the police would let us know if they had recovered them." Olivia plopped on the edge of the bed with a look of defeat as she lifted the phone to her ear. "I really hate to call them again."

"Call who?" Margaret asked as she entered the room with a sideways glance at her sister that would melt an ice cube.

"The police," her mother muttered with a deep sigh. "More of my jewelry is missing."

"I wonder who could have taken it." Margaret may as well have pointed an accusing finger at her sister—her implication was clear.

Trish gave her a "don't you dare say that out loud" glare. It would be just like her sister to try to blame it on her.

The three women froze at the sound of Wilmer's familiar *tap, tap, tap* as he appeared in the bedroom doorway.

"What are you three up to?" he asked with the usual scowl on his wrinkled face.

At first, none of the three responded.

"I—ah. My. . ." Olivia paused as if to choosing her words carefully.

"Just say it, woman!" Wilmer bellowed.

"I can't find my heart-shaped diamond brooch," she replied softly.

"What!" Wilmer stormed into the room and stood towering over his wife as she continued to sit on the bed's edge. "You've lost more jewelry?"

Olivia rose quickly to her feet and faced him squarely. "I have never *lost* my jewelry! Someone took it!"

Trish wished she were anywhere but in the room with her parents as the confrontation brewed.

"Are you saying someone reached in through a locked safe and removed your jewelry, Olivia?" Wilmer challenged with fire in his eyes as he glared at his wife.

"Of course not!" She crossed her arms over her chest and stood her ground defiantly. "That's a stupid thing to say!"

"Who would have the combination? Answer me that. Otherwise, how would they get into the safe without destroying it?"

"Apparently it's possible, Wilmer. It happened! The jewelry is gone!" his wife shouted at his supercilious expression.

Wilmer backed up a bit and with a point of his cane toward the phone, he ordered, "Call the police."

Detective Mercer arrived an hour later and assembled the entire household. Wilmer, Olivia, Margaret, Trish, Hildy, Anna, Martin, the chauffeur—they were all there. "As you know," he began as he eyed the little group, "this is the second time jewelry Mrs. Grayson says she has locked in her safe has disappeared. Do any of you have any idea who might have somehow learned the safe's combination? Or had an inordinate amount of time in Mrs. Grayson's room to have access to the safe?"

They each looked from one to another but no one answered.

"Let me ask another question, and I want each of you to think carefully. Have you seen anyone on the grounds, at any time, that gave you cause to question their presence? Someone who dressed like a workman? A repairman? Salesman? Maybe just someone loitering?"

"Impossible!" Wilmer barked out, as if offended by the idea. "That's why we have the electronic gate and a security system, to keep out unwanted intruders."

"Surely the front gate is not the only access to the grounds," the detective answered with a look of doubt toward the homeowner.

"Yes. The only one!"

"You mean to tell me there is no way someone could scale your fence?" Detective Mercer challenged.

Mr. Grayson gave him a disgusted look. "Maybe. But the man would have to be quite athletic to accomplish it."

"But it is possible, isn't it?" the determined investigator asked.

"I suppose," Wilmer conceded with a grunt.

The detective turned his attention to Olivia. "Have you checked to see if anything was missing beside your brooch?"

Olivia's hand went to her throat. "No—I haven't."

"Would you check it now, please? I need to know."

While Olivia went to check the safe's contents, the detective asked routine questions of the others still assembled, but stopped at the sudden reappearance of Mrs. Grayson, who was crying and looking terribly distraught.

"My marquise! It's gone, too. So is my diamond cocktail

ring!" She ran, nearly thrusting herself into her surprised husband's arms. "Who could've done this to me?"

"I don't know, Ma'am. But believe me, we're going to find out!" the detective stated with authority as he pulled the notebook from his pocket and began to write.

૱

"Mr. Ryan? Bart Ryan?"

Bart placed the bag of fertilizer on the potting table and turned to the stranger who'd walked up behind him. "Yes, sir," he answered with a friendly smile as he wiped his hand with the bandanna from his hip pocket. "What can I do for you?"

The man opened his billfold to show his identification. "I'm Detective Mercer, Mr. Ryan. I'd like to ask you a few questions."

"Sure. How about a coffee or cold drink while we talk? I'm afraid I've worked up a thirst." He motioned the man toward the little refreshment bar he kept for his customers' convenience. "What's your poison?"

"Coffee, thanks."

Bart filled their cups then shifted to one of the little round tables. "What's up?"

"Had a robbery at Grayson House—"

Bart gave him a startled look. "Another one?"

The detective's forehead creased. "You knew about the first one?"

Bart held his breath. Had he spoken too quickly? Would he have to confess his friendship with Trish? After all, that's where he'd heard about the jewelry's disappearance. "Yes. Seems someone mentioned it to me," he said, carefully weighing his words.

"I suppose bad news like that travels fast," the man answered, seeming satisfied. "Well, it's happened again. Some more pieces of very expensive jewelry have disappeared from the safe, and neither Mr. nor Mrs. Grayson has any idea how it could have happened."

"Um," Bart murmured as he sipped his cold drink. "So, what can I do to help?"

"Mr. Grayson gave me a list of persons and businesses who have regular access to Grayson grounds. Your name was on it. I need the names, addresses, and phone numbers of any of your staff who may have worked at Grayson House in the last three months."

Bart relaxed, glad Trish's name hadn't been mentioned. "Give me a sec and I'll have my secretary run one off for you. Anything else I can do for you?"

"No, unless you've seen anything unusual while you were there yourself, anything you think might seem worth checking out."

Bart gave it some thought. "Can't think of anything off-hand, but if anything occurs to me, I'll give you a call."

The detective waited, drinking his coffee while Bart went to his office and retrieved the list.

"I was wondering, Mr. Ryan—"

"Call me Bart."

The man smiled and began again. "I've been thinking, Bart. You and your men work the estate on a regular basis and probably know it as well as anyone. Mr. Grayson seems to think everything is well secured. Do you know of any place on the grounds where one might have easy access, other than the entry gate?"

Bart rubbed his chin. "I'm sure a guy could get in, if he really wanted to. The fence isn't that high." *Even my boys can get over it without much trouble.*

"Thanks. I'll call you if I have any further questions."

He was relieved when Detective Mercer rose to leave. "Want to take a pretty red geranium home to the missus? Compliments of Ryan Garden and Landscape!"

The man shook his head. "Tempting! She'd love it, but she'd probably think I'd been up to something. Besides, the police department might consider it payola. Thanks for the offer, but I'd better pass."

"Your call!" Bart gave the man's hand a hearty shake. "Good luck with your investigation."

"I'll need it! Didn't get too far the last time."

Bart watched as the man left the greenhouse and climbed into his unmarked car. Surely, Trish wasn't a suspect.

❧

Trish grabbed the phone on the first ring.

"Don't hang up. It's me!"

"Bart. What am I going to do with you? I told you to stay away from me."

"I know," he replied softly. "I'm trying, but I needed to talk to you. For two perfectly legitimate reasons."

She'd missed him already. It was nice to hear his voice.

"First, I have to know how you're doing. I heard there was another robbery at Grayson House."

She stiffened. "How did you hear that? They just discovered it this morning."

"A detective was just here. He told me."

"Why would he want to talk to you? I don't understand!"

"Routine. Don't worry. Only wanted to know if I was aware of any easy access to the grounds, since keeping the grounds is my company's responsibility. That's all. I called to see if they'd questioned you again."

"Yes. Everyone who works at the house."

"I suppose your parents are pretty upset."

"Upset? That's an understatement. My father was furious with my mother and accused her of being careless. She was livid!"

"But no one blamed you? I was concerned. I didn't want them to upset you."

She frowned. "Me? No. Why would they? I don't even know the safe's combination."

"No reason. I was afraid they might grasp at straws."

"No, they haven't. Not yet, anyway." She leaned into the couch's soft back and rubbed her hand over her belly. "What was the other reason?"

"I—ah, wondered when you had your next doctor's appointment."

"Bart," she chastised, "you are not supposed to be worrying about such things any longer."

"But I am, Trish. You're important to me!"

"You are a wonderful, caring man, and I praise the Lord for sending you into my life when I needed you so badly."

"You don't need me now?"

She took a deep breath and closed her eyes, visualizing the handsome man on the other end of the line. "Yes, I need you. I just can't allow myself the luxury of reaching out to you."

"I need you, too. I miss you like crazy."

"But—we can't—"

"We have to. . . ."

She closed her eyes as she listened to his pleas. How could she feel such an ache in her heart when she was separated from him like this? It had to be the hormonal imbalance of her pregnancy. Surely nothing more.

"Trish? Are you still there?"

"Yes," she whispered. "I'm here."

"Then listen to me. I don't want you driving to Denver in that station wagon. I'm going to take you to your doctor's appointment. It's tomorrow, isn't it?"

"Yes, one o'clock. I have the afternoon off."

"Drive to the parking lot of that grocery store on Third Street at noon and park in the lot. I'll be parked in my SUV on the street waiting for you. Not the pickup. We won't be so obvious that way. Oh, and ask Hildy if she minds if we get back late. I want to take you to a late lunch after your appointment, to make sure you get your veggies!"

"But—"

"Remember? No buts. Bart has spoken!"

She paused before answering, wanting to say yes, but needing to say no. "Are you sure it—"

"I'm sure. Please, Trish. You shouldn't be on the road in that car. I'd loan you mine, but I'd rather drive you. You know how bad the traffic can be."

She did hate the drive into Denver. The traffic always made her tense. "Okay. If you're sure you can take the time off from your business—"

"Trish! Of course I can take the time off. I'm the boss."

His voice was so kind, what else could she say? "I'll be there straight up noon. Thank you, Bart."

"No thanks necessary. It'll be my pleasure. I want that little boy to arrive safe and sound and healthy!"

She couldn't mask a snicker. "Boy? You mean girl, don't you?"

"I hope you're not planning on a dainty little girl. That little kicker is a boy!" he said with amusement. "Listen to ol' Bart. The voice of experience."

She giggled. "See you tomorrow."

"You'd better! Bye."

The parking lot was nearly full when Trish turned in off Third Street, but she found a place near the store's entrance. The SUV was parked in the street, right where he said it would be. The driver was smiling at her as she entered the passenger side.

"Wanted to open the door for you, but figured it'd be better if I didn't." Bart patted her shoulder then pulled away from the curb and headed toward Denver. "Have any trouble getting away?"

Trish shifted her purse from her shoulder to her lap. "None at all. Fortunately, Mother was lunching at a friend's house and had an afternoon of bridge planned."

"So, we can have that late lunch after your appointment?" he queried with a smile that made her heart rejoice.

"Yep, if the invitation still stands."

The drive to Denver seemed to take no time at all as the two rode along, visiting pleasantly about their children and their antics, the church, Bart's business, and the Graysons.

"Hold it!" Bart ordered at they pulled up at the curb of the free clinic. "No one is looking now. Let me get that door."

Trish turned when she realized he was following her into the clinic. "You're not going in, are you?"

"Of course I am."

"No, you can't!"

"Oh, but I can!" he answered as he caught up with her and his hand cupped her elbow. "No one knows us here. Stop worrying!"

She started to protest but realized it was in vain and, with a smile of surrender, allowed him to open the door for her.

"Mrs. Taylor, the doctor is ready for you; you may go on in," the receptionist instructed as Trish checked in at the little window. "Mr. Taylor," she added with a glance toward Bart, "You may go in with her if you like."

Trish let out a startled gasp, but Bart returned a big, toothy grin toward the woman. "No thanks, ma'am. I'll just look at one of those magazines while my *wife* talks with the doctor."

With a muffled snicker, Trish entered the office.

"Everything appears to be fine," Dr. Brewer said as she made a few new entries on her patient's chart. "Baby is doing fine, and from the looks of everything, so are you. Taking your vitamins?"

Trish nodded.

"Good. I'll need to see you in three weeks. Keep doing what you're doing, but I must emphasize—avoid stress!"

When Trish entered the waiting room, there was Bart, his

long legs sticking out in front of him, reading a magazine on child care. "All done!"

He dropped the magazine onto the table and jumped to his feet. "The boy doing okay?"

"*She* is doing fine!"

He gave her a mischievous grin as he herded her out the door toward the SUV. "When is she gonna take one of those tests? To let you know for sure it's a boy!"

"Don't you ever give up?"

"Not when it's a sure thing, and this baby's a boy! I know it!"

"You're incorrigible!"

"I'm also hungry! Let's eat!"

The steak house was crowded when they entered, but the greeter soon found them a table for two in a far corner, in the nonsmoking section.

"I'll just have the house salad." Trish folded the menu and handed it to the waiter.

"No, she won't! Give us both the number four and iced tea, done medium-well. And we'll have the steamed vegetables on the side," Bart ordered with authority.

"Bart! I couldn't possibly eat that much!"

"Try! That boy you're carryin' needs nourishment!"

"Oh, no!" Trish cried out as her palm flattened over her heart and her eyes focused on the opposite side of the restaurant. "I can't believe it!"

"What?" Bart asked, turning in his seat to see what had caught her attention.

eight

"It's Mother! Over there in the smoking section, in the corner."

"It's her all right."

"What'll we do? I don't want her to see us!"

"Let's scoot across the aisle. She won't be able to see us from there. That big plant is in the way. The waiter won't care."

Trish looked around nervously. "You sure?"

"Customer's always right! Remember?"

The two cautiously crossed to the little table, carrying their drinks, silverware, and napkins with them.

"Who's she with?"

Trish twisted in her seat and peered through the palm fronds. "Don't know. Never saw him before."

"Well, whoever he is, they sure don't look like they're enjoying their lunch. I'd say they're arguing about something, and pretty heatedly."

"Sure looks like it. Mother looks like she's about ready to explode!"

"I thought you said she was having lunch at a friend's house? With an afternoon of bridge."

"I did."

The waiter brought their salads, but a loud voice in the opposite corner of the restaurant drew their attention before they could take the first bite.

It was Olivia's, and she was on her feet, shouting something at the man seated at her table. He said something back, and in response Olivia's hand shot out and slapped the man hard across the face, then she indignantly stomped out of the restaurant.

"What was that all about?" Bart asked as he rubbed his chin and his eyes widened.

"I have no idea. But I'd sure like to know."

"Too bad you can't ask her when you get home."

"And let her know I've been in Denver with you? I think not!"

As they consumed their salads, the couple talked of many things, but the conversation kept finding its way back to Olivia and her unknown luncheon companion, who had also left the steak house.

"I can't imagine what that was all about, can you?" Trish quizzed as she picked up her roll.

"Me, either. Course, I don't know your mother well enough to know who her friends are."

"Friend? I don't think they looked like friends! My mother is pretty vain. She'd never put on a public display like that—unless she was angry enough to forget her surroundings. And," she said with great concern, "I don't think she even gave her surroundings a thought when she slapped that guy."

"What do you suppose he said, or did, to make her mad enough to slap him?"

"I can't imagine," Trish responded. She'd never seen her mother slap her father, no matter how angry he made her. No matter what the man had said, she could find no explanation for her mother's unorthodox behavior.

Bart slid his hand across the table and entwined his fingers with hers. "Let's forget about her, Trish."

She took a deep, cleansing breath. "I'll try."

His fingers tightened around hers. "I've got something to say."

She gazed into his dark eyes. "What?"

He gave her a sheepish grin. "About that kiss I stole. . ."

"Yes."

"I think maybe I owe you an apology. I kinda overstepped my bounds."

"You don't need to apologize. It was as much my fault as yours." She glanced away, feeling very foolish.

"You? No way! You didn't even know it was coming! I—just couldn't help myself. I had to kiss you."

"I—wanted you to kiss me."

His eyes grew wide. "You did?"

"Uh-huh. I know I had no business even thinking about—"

"You really did? You wanted me to kiss you?"

"Yes." Her answer was nothing more than a whisper.

Bart leaned forward, still holding her hand in his. "Oh, Trish, I never expected it to happen again—after Charlotte. But—I—think I may be falling in love with you."

She pulled her hand away from his. "You can't! We can't!" she said firmly as she leaned back in her chair. "I'm pregnant!"

"What's that got to do with it, Trish?"

"Bart! I have three children and another child on the way. No man in his right mind would fall in love with me!" she replied adamantly.

He made a crazy face and gave her a robust laugh. "Who said I was sane?"

"Be serious. I appreciate you taking me to the doctor today, but we have to end this. I can't have you putting yourself on the line like this. Do you know what would have happened if my mother had seen us together? My options are few. If my parents told me to leave—"

"I told you I'd never—"

"Bart!" She grasped his wrist to show him how serious she was. "My children and I are not your responsibility! I made my choice thirteen years ago with Jake, and I'm living with that decision. You're a wonderful man. You would do the same for any Christian woman in my circumstance. That's the kind of man you are. Don't confuse sympathy with. . ." She paused awkwardly, unable to voice the word she longed to say.

"Love, Trish?"

She pressed her finger to his lips. "Don't say that word. No more discussion on this—please! Let's enjoy our lunch and go home."

ﾊ

When Trish entered the house to help Hildy prepare breakfast the next morning, her mother was standing in the hallway. She couldn't resist and asked, "How was your luncheon yesterday?"

Olivia rotated her shoulders. "Fine."

"And your bridge game? Did you win any prizes?"

Her mother gave her a frown. "It was—enjoyable, and yes, I won a few trinkets. Why do you ask?"

"No reason," Trish answered as she moved past her into the kitchen.

Trish gave Hildy a quick squeeze about her shoulders as she entered. "Thanks again, Hildy, for watching the girls while I went to the doctor."

"Hey, you know how I love those girls. Babysitting them is pure pleasure. And with your mama off to play cards with her friends, I didn't even have to worry about her asking about you."

Trish pulled a whisk from a crock on the counter and began whisking the eggs vigorously. "Hildy, you've been around my folks as much as anyone. Do you think they're happy? With each other, I mean. They've been married for so long—"

"Whatcha asking, honey?" Hildy placed the pot of water on the range and stared at her.

Trish stopped whisking and gazed off into space. "They never seem to do anything together, unless it's for a social or business commitment. And my father seems so. . .cranky all the time."

"I think some of it is his health. He's slowed down a lot these past few years. And your mother is younger than he is. Maybe he just can't keep up with her anymore."

Trish pondered Hildy's speculation. Olivia *was* always on the go, flitting from one place to the next, serving on endless committees or playing golf and tennis. Her father rarely did anything physical. Maybe they no longer had anything in common. A worrisome thought struck her. Surely her mother wasn't having an affair with the man in the restaurant! Could what they witnessed have been a lover's quarrel?

❧

Trish wiped her eyes on her sleeve as the school bus headed down the road with her two precious daughters on board.

"Are we ready to go to work now, Mama?" little Zana asked as she jumped up and down with excitement.

Trish watched her baby with a heart full of love. "Yes, baby, it's time for us to go to work."

Late that afternoon, Detective Mercer showed up with a few more questions, but his investigation seemed to be running into a brick wall.

"Seems to me if you folks at the police department would quit eating doughnuts and do a little more investigating, you'd figure out who stole my wife's jewelry," Wilmer Grayson boomed at the man. "It's obvious the jewelry was stolen by someone who knew how to get into that safe without the combination. I've heard about professional safecrackers. Why don't you start with them? Don't you have a file on people like that?"

"Because," the detective said in an even tone, as if trying to contain his irritation with the man, "so far, everything points to an inside job."

Wilmer turned his full attention to the officer. "And what do you mean by that?"

"I mean, it appears someone knew the combination or knew where to find it, or someone knew they would have enough uninterrupted time to get it open without being discovered."

Mr. Grayson gave the man a holier-than-thou look. "Young man, are you implying—"

"Sir," the detective answered without backing down, "I am not implying anything. Merely investigating your robbery. I'd like to talk to your daughter."

Wilmer appeared puzzled. "Daughter?"

"Yes, Margaret."

"Why? She doesn't know anything."

"Because, sir, there are only three people who know the combination to that safe. You, your wife, and your daughter. It's highly unlikely that you or your wife would have given the combination to anyone. Perhaps your daughter—"

"My daughter what?" Wilmer asked, his hackles up as he glared at the man.

"I was about to say, perhaps your daughter had the combination written down somewhere—a notebook, a sticky note. Maybe one of her acquaintances saw it or found it."

"Never! Margaret is a competent young woman. She is responsible for hundreds of thousands of dollars as the administrator of Grayson Foundation. She would never be that careless. And I resent your accusations. Rest assured, the police chief will hear about this."

Detective Mercer took a deep breath and let it escape slowly. "Call me if you think of anything I should know. In the meantime, I'd like to talk to Margaret—privately."

Trish was listening from the dining room where she was polishing the silver tea set. In his investigation, would he find out the Graysons had another daughter? If so, would she become a suspect?

She continued polishing as she heard Margaret enter the living room and the detective begin his questioning. She almost felt sorry for her sister as his questions pried into her private life. Even though Margaret had gone out of her way to make Trish's life miserable, she was confident her sister had nothing to do with the missing jewelry. But who did?

The polishing finished, she moved into the kitchen, fearing someone would discover her in the dining room and accuse her of eavesdropping.

She'd barely put the polish and cleaning cloths into the cabinet when the door to the hall opened and her father entered.

"Trish!" he barked in his usual harsh tone. "Detective Mercer would like to talk to you."

Trish pulled on her sweater, smoothed her hair, lifted her chin, and followed her father into the grand foyer where the detective was waiting for them.

"Good morning, Mrs. Taylor," he said pleasantly as he moved forward to greet her.

"Good morning," she responded, pulling her sweater about her to cover her now protruding abdomen.

The man pulled out his notebook, checked a few pages and asked, "Do you know Bart Ryan, Mrs. Taylor?"

Trish's heart drummed against her chest. "Yes, sir, I know him. He and his crew work on the grounds regularly."

"I understand you live in the caretaker's cabin, right here on the estate, is that correct?"

"Yes. It is," she confirmed.

"Mr. Ryan has told us there are places along the fence between this property and the Kirkwood estate where someone athletic could gain access. Since the caretaker's cabin is beyond the grove and you have a better view of the back half of the estate, I wonder if you've seen anyone in the area at odd times, times when you normally wouldn't expect them to be here. Like weekends or evenings?"

Bart told him that? Of course, he told him. He would never lie when asked a direct question.

"Mrs. Taylor?"

"Sorry, I was thinking." She paused. "No one other than

Mr. Ryan and his crew, but you already know about them."

"Okay," he said slowly as he made an entry in his book. "One more question. Have you at anytime been in Mrs. Grayson's bedroom when her safe was open?"

"Yes, sir. Just once. I was in her bathroom, putting towels away, the second time she discovered jewelry was missing from her safe."

"Are you through with her?" Wilmer asked impatiently as he leaned on his cane.

"Yes, for now." The policeman closed the little book and slipped it into his pocket. "Thank you, Mrs. Taylor. I won't keep you any longer."

Trish backed away with a forced smile and returned to the kitchen where a bag of vegetables waited to be cleaned and peeled. A blast of fear chilled through her. Perhaps she hadn't been as alarmed about the robbery as she should've been. Whoever took those pieces had somehow gotten access to the grounds, the very grounds where she and her daughters lived. Until now, she hadn't felt threatened. There certainly wasn't anything in the caretaker's cabin that would be worth stealing. Except. . . Her blood ran cold at the thought and she drew her sweater closer about her. Her and her children! Someone deranged enough to break into a house and steal may have no qualms about molesting women and children if the opportunity presented itself!

"Trish, could you take this up to your mother for me?" Hildy asked as she placed a tall glass of iced tea and a napkin on the tray. "She wanted it right away."

"Sure," she answered, relieved to have her frightening thoughts interrupted. "Be glad to."

Olivia was sitting in front of her mirror staring at her reflection when her daughter entered. "Patricia, do you think I look old?" she asked with in an almost melancholy tone as she squinted and critically scanned her appearance.

Trish placed the tray on the table and moved to her mother's side. "Of course not, Mother. No one would ever guess that you're as old as you are."

"As old as I am? What does that mean?" Olivia asked as she glared at her daughter's reflection.

Trish wished she could swallow her previous words, acutely aware of her mother's vanity. "What I meant, Mother, was that you look so much younger than you really are. No one would ever be able to accurately guess your age." And she meant it. Olivia did look several years younger than what her birth certificate stated.

"Patricia, take off that sweater," her mother instructed as she left her vanity and removed a hanger from her closet. "I was going to give this jacket to the Junior League sale, but I think it will fit you just fine."

Trish stood stock-still as panic seized her. "I—ah. . ." Her mind searched for an excuse to avoid removing the sweater that was masking the enlarged abdomen she'd so cautiously concealed. "I—really don't need a jacket, Mother. I—"

"Of course, you need a jacket! You wear that same old sweater every day. This will look much nicer than that baggy sweater." Olivia thrust the jacket toward her. "Here, try it on."

Trish had been searching for the proper way to tell her mother about her pregnancy and had discovered there was no right way, or right time, and began to slowly remove the sweater.

Olivia's eyes rounded and she gasped. "Trish! You're pregnant!"

nine

Trish took a deep, cleansing breath and allowed her stomach muscles to relax. No point in holding it in—her secret was out.

"How, Patricia? I mean—who?" Olivia sank onto the edge of her bed, her gaze glued to the obvious bulge dominating her daughter's otherwise slender frame.

She quickly tugged the sweater back on and crossed her arms protectively over the mound. "Who, Mother? Jake, of course! How dare you think otherwise!"

"Oh, Patricia, how could you do this to us a second time?"

Trish gave her a dubious look. "To you, Mother? What have I done to you?"

"Embarrass us like this!"

Trish's hands went to her hips as she glared at her mother, amazed and chagrined by Olivia's foolish questions. Did her mother ever think of anything but her precious reputation? "Embarrass you? How could I embarrass you? No one even knows your prodigal daughter has returned home. You've kept me under wraps since I arrived, remember? I'm your servant. How could I embarrass you when people don't even know I'm related to you?"

Olivia gave her daughter a haughty look. "It's bound to come out, Patricia. Things like that always do!" Her gaze moved to her daughter's abdomen again. "Just how long did you think you could hide it?"

"I never wanted to hide my pregnancy, Mother. I'm proud to be carrying Jake's baby. I loved him very much."

"How far along are you?"

"Five months," Trish confessed, her heart beating wildly.

"Five months?" her mother screamed as she rose to her feet. "Why, Patricia, didn't you have an abortion when you found out you were pregnant? Before you came to Grayson House? Is that why Jake killed himself? He didn't want any more children to feed?"

Trish gritted her teeth and clenched her fists. "Mother! You didn't know your son-in-law at all! Jake loved our children—and being a daddy. You know I would never have an abortion. Surely you remember how I feel about that. As I recall, we had this same conversation thirteen years ago. And for your information, I didn't find out I was pregnant until after I arrived at Grayson House! If I'd known, I'd never have come here, even if it meant going on welfare. Your reaction is exactly what I expected it would be." Her knees felt weak and her hands were shaking as she stood facing her mother. The moment of truth she'd been dreading had arrived.

"Your father is not going to be happy when he hears this news, Patricia. You have no idea how furious he was with you the first time—"

Trish stepped toward her mother, her palms open and extended in question. "First time? You make it sound like I've done something terrible. This is my husband's baby, Mother. What is so wrong about that?"

"What's wrong with what?" Wilmer stormed into his wife's room, his cane tapping his entrance. "I could hear you two clear down the hall. What have you done to upset your mother?"

Trish did a double take as she turned to face her father. "Me? Upset her? It's—"

"She's pregnant. Wilmer! Pregnant, can you believe it?"

Wilmer stared, his eyes wide. "You're pregnant, Patricia? Again?" His glare rested on her abdomen. "You *are* pregnant!"

Trish stood proudly, her shoulders erect, her head held high. "Yes, Father. I am."

"She says it's Jake's child," Olivia volunteered with a half smirk.

Her father's beady eyes squinted and he frowned. "Why didn't you tell us when you arrived, Patricia? Didn't you think we deserved to know, taking you and those children in like we did?"

Trish chose her words carefully, knowing her children's welfare was at stake, more now than ever, and answered calmly. "I didn't know, Father, until after I'd arrived. I went to the doctor and she said I was—"

Olivia grabbed her daughter by the wrist. "You've been to a doctor? Here in Cedar Ridge?"

"I went the doctor—"

"Oh, Wilmer," Olivia said, turning to her husband, "the whole town will know. Whatever will they think?"

Trish pulled her arm away. "If you'd let me finish, you'd know the doctor I went to was in Denver, not Cedar Ridge. Give me a little credit. I'm smarter than that!"

Her mother breathed a deep sigh and moved to Wilmer's side before confronting her daughter again. "That only buys us a little time. Our friends must not find out about this."

"You can't expect to keep these kinds of things quiet. They have a way of getting out. People talk." Her father threw a sour look toward Trish. "And we've barely gotten over the embarrassment of your last fiasco."

Olivia quickly looked at her husband. "Do you think we can trust the servants to keep quiet?"

Wilmer nodded his head confidently. "If they want to keep their jobs they'll keep quiet."

"Hey, you two!" Trish shouted. "This baby is going to be born. You can't hide something like that forever. Nor do I want to!"

Her father gave her a harsh stare. "You be quiet, young lady. You are in no position to be belligerent with us, unless your financial status has somehow magically turned for the better since you arrived on our doorstep with those three children. Penniless and without a roof over your head or food to eat." His voice was sharp and degrading. "Your mother and I will discuss your predicament and let you know when we have decided how to handle it."

"Handle it? This is my baby, you know. Shouldn't I have some say in this?"

Wilmer gave one of his famous snorts. "Not as long as I'm paying the bills, you don't. My reaction, right now, is to send you packing, Patricia. But there are other people in this equation. Us, and your children."

"Yes, Patricia. You should've thought of those three children before you went and got yourself pregnant again."

"I didn't go and get myself pregnant again, as you put it. This baby is the result of the love of two people who cared very much for one another. My husband's baby," Trish retorted, her control nearly shattered.

"Your *dead* husband's baby, may I remind you, young lady. He is not the one taking care of you now. I am!" Wilmer boasted with a thump of his cane.

Trish blinked hard, trying to regain her composure. "Yes, you are, Father. And I am grateful. However, I plan to pay you back. I don't know how or when, but if you will allow me to stay until my baby is born, I'll get a job and move out as soon as I'm back on my feet." She patted her abdomen lovingly. "Right now, I'm sure no one would hire me. But after this baby arrives, I'll be able to get a job and take care of my family myself."

"Without a college education? A job paying enough to feed, clothe, and house four children plus yourself? I don't think so, missy. Get serious! You're dreaming—something you always did very well, I might add."

Trish gave a shrug of her shoulders, knowing her next statement would infuriate her proud father. "Well, there's always welfare! I'm sure I'd qualify."

Olivia jumped to her feet. "You wouldn't! Not welfare!"

"I might, if I were desperate enough. If you kicked me out."

"Your mother and I will discuss it, Patricia. We'll let you know when we've reached a solution to this problem."

"This is not a problem to be solved, Father. It's a baby!" Trish reminded him as she closed the door behind her.

⋆

The big yellow school bus rolled up to the Grayson House gate right on time and Trish and Zana were waiting as two giggling girls stepped off, their lunch buckets swinging from their hands.

"So, how was it?" Trish quizzed as she tugged her coat closer across her chest to ward off the chilling winds.

"Good. I like this school and I've got the neatest teacher and—"

"I saw Kyle," Kari said, her eyes dancing with excitement. "He goes to my school. He said he misses me."

"Kyle goes to your school?" her mother questioned in surprise.

"Uh-huh," Kari confirmed, "he does. And I saw Bart, too. He was waiting in his truck after school, with Andy."

"Did he—ask about me?" Trish asked casually, pleased at the mention of her friend's name.

"He told me to tell you that you'd be hearing from him soon. Mama, does that mean they're going to come and see us?"

She shook her head. " 'Fraid not, honey."

"Don't they like us anymore?" Kari asked as her face curled up in a frown.

"Of course, they like us."

She'd never tell the girls, but she missed Bart much more than they did. There was barely a waking moment in her day she didn't think of him, wishing she could pick up the phone and call him. But that was impossible. She meant nothing but trouble for the man who'd befriended her, especially now that her secret was out.

"I want Zeb to come and play Candyland with me," Zana pleaded as she tugged on her mother's hand. "Can we call him and ask him to come over?"

Trish shook her head sadly. "No, baby. We can't."

"But why?"

"Yeah, why?" Kerel asked as the little group walked briskly toward the caretaker's cabin. "I want to go to their church again."

"You'll like a new church, once you get used to it, sweetie."

"But, Mom, I liked my Sunday school teacher at the Ryans' church. And the kids were real friendly. Do we have to go to a new church?" Kerel begged as she adjusted the shoulder strap on her book bag.

"Sorry, kids. That's just the way it is. Remember, God's presence isn't in just one church. There are many churches that preach His Word. Now, let's have no more discussion on this. Maybe someday we can go back and visit the Ryans' church again, okay?"

After the dinner dishes had been cleaned up and the children tucked into bed for the night, Trish settled down in the old frieze recliner to work on her quilt. There was something relaxing about piecing the little trapezoids together and seeing the pattern take shape as a Christian radio station played softly in the background.

She smiled contentedly and massaged her palm across the firm roundness of her abdomen. Funny, since her parents had learned of her pregnancy, the baby within her had begun to kick more and move around more, as if it were suddenly granted freedom to expand, no longer having to limit its movement under the bulky sweater of concealment.

A slight noise outside on the porch made her heart clench. Since the detective's last visit and his words of caution, she'd made sure the doors and windows on the little cabin were locked securely at all times. Motionless, she sat listening for the slightest sound, her heart pounding with fear.

There was a slight rap, then her muffled name. "Trish, it's me. Bart."

Nearly leaping from her place in the chair, she moved quickly to the door and flung it open to her late-night caller. "Bart? What are you doing here?"

"I'm alone. Can I come in?"

"Of course. Come in," she said eagerly, glad to see his smiling face.

He stepped inside, shutting the door behind him as he pulled his ball cap from his head. "I—had to see you. To make sure you were okay."

"I'm fine, Bart. Things have been a little harried around here today, but so far, I'm okay."

He took her hand and gently rubbed his cool thumbs across her knuckles. "You're sure? And what about the little boy? He's okay?"

She laughed aloud, momentarily forgetting about the sleeping children in the adjoining bedrooms so near to where they were standing. "You never give up, do you?"

"Why should I?" he said with his infectious grin. "I know it's gonna be a boy. Still kickin' hard, isn't he?" He lifted her hands to his lips and kissed them as he gazed into her eyes. "I've missed you, Trish."

"I've missed you, too," she admitted. "So have the girls. Just today, they asked why we couldn't go to your church."

"What'd you tell them?"

She tilted her head slightly. "Just that we couldn't. Oh, Bart. You know we can't see each another. Especially not after today."

"Today? What happened today?" he asked as a deep frown creased his forehead.

"They know I'm pregnant." She pulled him toward the sofa and seated herself, then motioned him to the cushion next to her.

"Oh, Trish. How'd you tell them?" he asked as his arm slipped around her shoulders.

"I didn't have to tell them. Mother saw—I'm getting too big to hide it." She lovingly placed her palm over her rounded abdomen.

"But you're still here. They didn't throw you out like you expected they would. That has to be a good sign."

She leaned into his shoulder, needing to draw from his strength. "Not yet. Maybe tomorrow. They haven't decided yet. They're talking it over."

"Unbelievable!" he exclaimed as his fingers moved to knead her tense shoulders. "I'd hate to have those two making decisions about my life!"

"They will be, if they discover you're with me." She straightened. "You know you shouldn't be here. My neck is on the chopping block. I don't want to see yours there, too. You'd better go."

He pulled her back into the curve of his arm. "Don't you worry about me, my sweet. I was making a good living before I got the Grayson contract, and if necessary, I can do without it."

"You stubborn man. Don't you see? Our friendship means enough to me that I am willing to do without it rather than have you or your business suffer because of me."

His hand cupped her chin as he lifted her face to his. "Let me do the worrying, okay? I know the risk I'm taking. I refuse to stay away from you because of what might happen to me. But I *will* stay away from you if it means you'll get hurt *because* of me. There's a difference. They can't hurt me.

But they can hurt you, and I won't be the reason!"

The clock on the little table ticked loudly as the two sat silently. Trish stole a look at Bart and found his gaze locked on hers. "Bart. . ."

"What is it, Trish?"

"Nothing. You should go."

"Go? I haven't told you why I came here tonight. Don't you want to hear?" He lowered his voice with a glance toward the little bedrooms where the children lay sleeping.

"I have good news. I talked to Dr. Hancock. He's in my Bible study group. I told him all about you and—"

"Me? You told someone in Cedar Ridge about my pregnancy? Oh, Bart. How could you?"

His fingers entwined with hers. "Trish, in confidence. He won't tell anyone. Anyway, I told him about you, and he has agreed to take you on as a patient. You won't have to drive to Denver anymore. And, he's the finest obstetrician in the area."

She gave him a look of skepticism. "I can't afford—"

"That's the best part. It's pro bono. No charge. He takes on several pro bono cases each year, as a service to the Lord, and he wants to be your doctor. Isn't that good news?"

She massaged her forehead wearily. "I'm not a charity case, Bart."

"Trish! Didn't you hear what I said? This isn't charity. He does it for the Lord. Would you deprive him of that service?"

She looked thoughtful, then questioned, "You're not paying for this?"

"No. Scout's honor."

"Umm. Okay, if you're sure," she said gratefully. "Please convey my gratitude to Dr. Hancock."

"I've already set up your first appointment." He grinned confidently as he handed her a little card with the doctor's address and her appointment time on it.

She looked at the man seated next to her and marveled at his concern for her and her family. "Thank you, Bart. You're the greatest."

"I'll do anything to make your life easier, Trish. You know that," he said as he rose to go. "Anything." He held her hand as they walked the few steps to the door.

"You'll never know how much it means to me to have a friend like you."

He opened the door with his free hand and stood in the coolness of the evening air as it rushed past him.

She shivered slightly.

"Trish. . ."

She looked up into his face as he spoke.

"I. . ."

"Yes?"

"I. . ." Slowly, his head lowered and his lips brushed lightly across hers as he folded her into his arms.

"Bart. Don't," she murmured as she relaxed into the warmth of his embrace. "We shou—"

"Yes, we should," he whispered into her hair as his grip tightened around her and he drew her close.

"But," she whimpered as she pushed back slightly, "I'm pregnant."

"I know," he uttered as their lips met fully.

Trish told herself she couldn't let this happen. It was ridiculous! She'd become a widow only a few months ago. She was the mother of three children who were totally dependent upon her, and she had a fourth child due in a few months. No man would want to saddle himself with that situation, especially a man who had three children of his own to support. But, for the first time, she admitted to herself how much she'd longed to be held like this, kissed like this, by Bart Ryan. Now it was happening, and she couldn't find the strength to put a stop it.

"I had to kiss you, Trish. I've thought of nothing else since that first time—"

Her finger touched the tip of his nose and she smiled into his eager face. "You're crazy, Bart Ryan." She felt his lips brush hers again and she tingled from head to toe as she allowed herself to participate, her arms finding their way to encircle his strong neck. "I think we're both crazy."

"Hi, Bart." Little Zana's high-pitched voice startled the pair as she stood in the middle of the living room rubbing her sleepy eyes, her teddy bear tucked under her arm. "Did you come to see me?"

He crossed the room quickly and scooped Zana up in his arms. "I sure did, honey. Bart's missed his big girl."

Zana wrapped her arms around the late caller's neck and placed her head on his shoulder. "I love you, Bart," she said with a big yawn. "I'm tired. Would you tuck me in?"

"Sure," he said with a wink to her mother as he turned and disappeared into the darkened bedroom with the sleepy child.

"You're really something, Bart Ryan," Trish sighed as he came back into the room. "My girls think you're pretty special."

"And what do *you* think?" he asked as he pulled her to him once more.

"I think you'd better go."

He kissed her forehead, and then the tip of her nose.

She lifted her lips to his as his mouth sought hers. Their kiss was gentle, tender, precious.

"Trish," he whispered as they drew apart, their gazes locked on one another in the soft glow of the lamp on the end table. "You remind me of a dandelion. You know that?"

She scanned his face, smiling contentedly. "A dandelion?"

"Yes, a dandelion," he murmured with an easy chuckle. "No matter what happens to you, no matter how badly someone crushes you, you spring back, as resilient as ever, looking as bright and sunny as if nothing bad has ever happened to you.

You've been trampled on, and you've been jerked from your roots. How many times now? Yet you remain strong and determined to survive. No matter what the obstacles, you find your way around them and come up stronger each time. Yep," he said as he pushed a lock of hair from her forehead, "you're like a dandelion."

"Umm. A dandelion," she echoed as she cupped her hand over his. "I think I like that."

"You're my little dandelion."

Trish leaned her head against his chest, savoring their few minutes together. It was as though time stood still and they were off in another world filled with peace and harmony and love as they shared their special moment. No matter what the future held, this precious experience would live in her memory forever. And she'd be able to draw strength from it to go on, no matter what happened.

"If only it could be like this forever."

"Bart! You have to go!" she announced as she once again thought about the consequences to both of them if he were discovered in her cabin. She pushed away from his grasp. "As much I want to see you—I can't! Please understand. I have to be careful. I've asked my parents to allow me to stay here until after my baby is born."

"*He* is born," he said with a smile.

"*She* is born," she corrected. "I told them that if they would allow us to stay until then, I'll leave and get a job. I don't know who'd want to hire me, with no experience. And I'll have to make enough to support the five of us or we'll have to go on welfare. But right now, I can't do anything to alienate my parents, Bart. Like seeing you. You do understand, don't you?"

With a deep sigh, he nodded. "I don't like this, Trish. I want to be with you."

"I want to be with you, too. But—"

"I know."

"Then you'll agree? We'll avoid any contact? At least until I'm out of my parents' house. Then—"

"Then?"

She stood on tiptoes and kissed his cheek. "Then—we'll see. Meanwhile, please, stay out of my life. Okay?"

"I'll try," he agreed reluctantly with a sheepish grin. "But I'm not makin' any promises! And know I'll be praying for you. So will the boys." With a final quick kiss, Bart backed out the door and closed it behind him.

Trish touched her fingers to her lips, reveling in the thrill of his kiss. "Dandelion," she repeated with a smile. "Only Bart would think of that."

❧

With Kari and Kerel safely deposited on the school bus and Zana settled in, Trish reported to work in the kitchen.

"Hear anything from your folks yet?" Hildy asked as she sorted and picked through a huge carton of strawberries.

Trish shook her head as she tied an apron around her expanding waist. "Not yet. Oh, Hildy, what if they tell me I have to leave? Where will I go? And how will we ever live?"

The robust woman dried her hands on her apron and offered a reassuring hug to her friend and coworker. "Surely they wouldn't do that. You're their daughter, their flesh and blood."

The young woman breathed deeply. "I hope you're right. If I wasn't this far along, they'd probably demand an abortion for this baby, like they did when I was carrying Kerel."

"I wish I could do something to help."

Trish patted the cook's hand. "You already have, just by being you."

Martin gave the two women a searching look as he entered the kitchen and told Trish her parents were ready to see her.

"Well, this is it!" Trish groaned as she untied her apron and moved to the door. "Pray for me, Hildy."

Wilmer and Olivia sat side by side on the leather sofa, waiting, as their daughter entered the room and slid into the chair facing them. "Martin said you wanted to see me. Does this mean you've made a decision?"

ten

Wilmer studied his wayward daughter intently before answering. "This is not an easy situation for any of us."

"Especially your father and me!" Olivia confirmed quickly. "We've decided the only logical answer, the one that will cause the least ramifications, is for you to have an abortion. We have a doctor friend who—as a favor to us, even though it's late into your—"

"No! Absolutely not! I won't do it!"

The tip of Wilmer's cane rose and pointed toward her. "You listen to your mother, young lady. An abortion is the best solution to your problem. Think of your other children. For once, think of someone else, other than yourself!"

"Me, Father? That's a joke! I don't care one whit what happens to me. My children are all I ever think of. They're the only reason I came back to Grayson House to beg for your help." She stood to her feet, her body trembling with anger. "An abortion? Give up Jake's baby? No! I refuse. I'll go on welfare first!"

"Sit down!" her father ordered, his voice loud and harsh. "Your mother and I were afraid you'd refuse. We have an alternative plan. You'd better hear us out before you go storming out of here."

"Yes, Patricia," her mother added with a shudder. "We can't have a Grayson drawing government assistance. What would people think?"

Trish plopped back into the chair, fighting the urge to respond to her mother's vain comments. "What is this alternate plan?"

"Well," Wilmer began in his typical arrogant fashion, "you can't continue to work in the living areas of the house in your condition. Too many people from town and are in and out of here every day. So we, your mother and I, have decided, until the baby's birth, it would be best if you no longer worked at the house."

Trish tried to interrupt her father, but he raised his hand for silence, and she settled back into the chair.

"Stay in the cabin, and I will continue to pay you what I've been paying as your wages. And provide your food. Give your grocery list to Hildy each week, and she'll order it along with hers."

"I will pay you back, I promise." Trish was relieved to know she and her little family could stay, at least until the baby was born.

"No need to pay me back. I'm looking at this fiasco as a philanthropic project my foundation would take on if you weren't related to me. Of course, since you are related to me, it is not deductible as a charitable contribution, but I'll look at it as I would any other bad investment."

"Bad investment?" Trish queried, upset by his insult. "That's what I am to you, Father? A bad investment?"

"Don't mince words with me, Trish. You are in no position to quibble over terms. Think of your children before you say things you might regret."

She bit her tongue. He was right. He was offering her the best possible choice under the circumstances. She should be grateful. "Thank you, Father."

"And you'd better thank me, too," Olivia chimed in as if she thought she might miss an opportunity to receive credit due her. "We are being very generous with you, I hope you realize that."

"As long as you keep a low profile," Wilmer added to her mother's comment. "Our arrangement stands only as long as you abide by our rules. Other than activities at the children's school and your doctor appointments, we prefer that you remain at home. The more you are out in the community the more likely it is that someone will recognize you."

"Yes, Patricia. It took us years to overcome the shame you caused us the last time you turned up pregnant. Let's not have a repeat performance."

Trish glared at her mother, but said nothing.

"You may go now, Patricia." Her father gestured toward the door with his cane. "That is, if you agree to our terms."

Trish lifted her chin proudly as she stood to her feet. "I agree, Father. And thank you. Both."

≈

Bart was on his knees planting a vast array of colorful chrysanthemums in new flower bed edging the circle drive in front of Grayson House. He'd been at it most of the day, but his mind hadn't been on his task. It'd been on the decisions being made in the house by its owners. Each time someone entered or exited the house, his head had turned, hoping for a glimpse of the woman who'd come into his life.

He gathered the rakes, hoes, and the other tools he'd used, placed them in the back of his pickup, and climbed in behind the wheel. As he glanced in the rearview mirror, he saw the front door open and Wilmer Grayson and his wife appear, dressed as though they were going out for the evening. He watched as their chauffeur opened the limousine door for the couple.

Bart smiled to himself. If they were going out for the evening, it'd give him an opportunity to see Trish before he headed back to the nursery. He watched as the limo headed down the long drive and moved through the gate and out of sight before starting the engine and driving to the back of the big house, past the grove where he then parked, preferring to walk the rest of the way to the cabin.

"Hi," he said softly as he rounded the caretaker's cabin.

Trish was standing on the porch, her shawl wrapped around her to protect her from the late fall air. "You startled me," she responded with a welcoming smile. "I'm glad to see you, but you know you shouldn't be here."

"It's okay. They're gone. Your folks, I mean." He stepped onto the porch and took her hand in his. "I watched them go, and from the way they were dressed, they're out for the evening." He rotated his thumb across her knuckles as he held her hand. "So, how'd it go today? Get any answers?"

She gazed up into his eyes. "They're allowing the children and me to stay, at least until after the baby is born." After filling him in on the details of her meeting with her parents, she said, "Bart, if they knew you befriended me, they'd. . ."

"They'd what?"

"They'd take it out on both of us. I know them, Bart. Promise me, this time you'll stay away from me, please."

He pulled her into his arms. "I can't make a promise like that."

"Bart—"

"I *can't* stay away. I have to see you. Look, I have an idea. What if I come here late at night? After the children have gone to bed? I'll park over near the highway. I can scale the fence and follow the creek in through the grove. No one will see me."

"What if someone does?"

"No one will. I'll be careful. Please say yes, Trish. I just need to be with you, to see that you're okay."

She appeared thoughtful. "Well. . ." Her eyes widened. "What about your boys?"

"They'll be fine. I'll tell Zeb where I'll be. He knows how much I've missed you."

She nodded with a sigh. "Okay. I want to see you, too. Just promise you'll watch yourself. But if we're ever found out, we have to be honest and admit to what we've been doing."

He gave her a tender smile. "What have we been doing, Trish? Nothing we should be ashamed of. I'd be proud to tell the world about you. Your parents are the ones with the problem."

She nestled her face into his chest. "I hadn't thought of it that way."

"We're two grown adults, both single, both responsible. There's nothing tawdry or shameful in what we're doing. We aren't really deceiving anyone. We're just keeping our relationship discreet. God knows we don't want to hurt anyone. I'm more concerned about what He thinks than I am about old Wilmer Grayson."

She gazed up at him with admiration in her eyes. "My hero."

"I'd never let you down or betray you. You know that, don't you?"

She nodded.

"I'll come as often as I can."

"I'll be waiting for you," she murmured in a mere whisper.

Zana tapped on the window, waved her little hand, then pressed her face against the glass.

Her mother stiffened and pushed away from her visitor. "The children, Bart. They might not understand their mother in the arms of another man. It's been such a short time since they lost their father."

He waved at the tiny face in the window. "I'd better be going. I promised the boys I'd take them out for pizza tonight. Wish you and the girls could go with us, but I guess that's a bad idea, huh?"

She playfully jabbed him in the arm with her clenched fist. "Go. And tell your boys hello for us. And that we miss them, too. Maybe, someday—"

"No maybes, Trish. There is going to be a someday for us."

"We'll see." She watched him back down the steps.

"I'll knock three times when I come, so you'll know it's me!"

"Just hoot like an owl instead," she quipped.

❧

Trish tiptoed past Wilmer's study with the small box of personal items she'd accumulated during the time she'd worked as a servant in her parents' home, hoping she wouldn't be noticed. Out of curiosity, she paused as she passed the open doorway when she heard the voices of Detective Mercer and her parents.

"Your stolen jewelry turned up at three different pawnshops, all of them located within two hundred miles of Cedar Ridge."

"Well, this is a surprise," Wilmer mocked. "The police department finally got off its haunches and got to work. So, am I to assume you have found out who stole those pieces?"

Trish smiled. Her father's attitude was so predictable.

"No. We haven't. But it shouldn't be long. Those shop owners are at the station right now, going over the mug books. I have a feeling we'll have our man soon."

"You're sure it was my jewelry?" Olivia asked. Trish was surprised at the hysteria in her mother's voice. Usually Olivia took things in stride, letting others do the worrying and fretting, but she seemed unduly upset by the detective's news.

"Oh, it's your jewelry, all right. I'll need you to come down to the station and identify it, of course. But it's yours. No doubt about it. And the stupid guy who pawned it apparently did nothing to disguise his appearance. Can you believe that?"

"Then you'll soon have him in custody?" Wilmer asked.

"I'll let you know when we get him. Meantime, I'd like you both to come down and take a look at that jewelry."

Trish moved on along the hall, not wanting to be seen by either the detective or her parents. So, they'd found her mother's jewelry. That was good news. Maybe there'd be an arrest and things would return to normal.

૨ઢ

Dr. Hancock checked Trish's chart. "I'd say that baby is coming along real well. Your weight is in line and you seem to be taking reasonable care of yourself. You're still taking your vitamins? And doing a little walking every day?"

She smiled warmly at her new obstetrician. "Yes, Dr. Hancock. This is my fourth pregnancy. I have the drill down pat!"

He made a few notes then asked, "Want to know if it's a boy or a girl?"

She pondered his question. "No, I don't think so. Not knowing is half the fun."

"It's up to you, but I'm inclined to agree with you. My wife and I didn't want to know either."

She grew serious. "I need to ask you something, Dr. Hancock."

He stopped writing. "Sure. What is it?"

She twisted nervously on the paper sheet, causing a crinkling sound. "About your pay. . ."

He put a reassuring hand on her shoulder. "Now, don't you go worrying about that. It's all been taken care of."

"But I need to know. Bart said you were taking me on as a pro bono case. Is that true?"

He gave her a shy grin. "Yes. I'll be honest with you. Bart insisted on paying for my services, but I offered to take you on pro bono when he told me your story."

She stiffened. "My story?"

"I recognized your name when Bart told me you were Trish Taylor. Jake used to work on my car. I knew that young man very well. Good mechanic and as honest as they come. I remember the scandal it caused when news spread that you were pregnant and ran off to marry Jake. I respected you for not having an abortion, which is what I understood your parents wanted you to do, and Jake for standing by you. You see,

I already knew you were a Grayson. I've dealt with your parents before. No offense, Trish, but my dealings with them have not been pleasant."

"And you took me on anyway?" she asked, slightly embarrassed.

"I took you on because I knew Jake. And Bart said you are a fine mother and a Christian. I was there when you and your girls visited our church service with the Ryan family. As a fellow Christian, I am doing this not only for you but also for the Lord. It's one way I can serve Him. Now, I want you to stop at the reception desk on your way out and make your next appointment. I need to see you in three weeks."

As Trish crawled into the old station wagon, she lowered her head and thanked the Lord for sending Bart into her life. It was as if he'd been sent by God Himself, as her guardian angel. Everything good that had happened to her since she'd arrived in Cedar Ridge had happened because of Bart. Including Dr. Hancock.

࿐

Fall had long since arrived with its cooler days and longer nights. Leaves fell from the trees, heralding the impending arrival of winter. Other than regular late-night visits from Bart and her appointments with Dr. Hancock, life was pretty routine on the Grayson estate for the Taylor family.

December came in with a blast of cold from the north, and Cedar Ridge was blanketed with a foot of pristine white snow. The caretaker's cabin was warm and cozy, and other than making occasional trips to the house to see Hildy when the Graysons were out, Trish stayed close to home. With the baby due in slightly over a month, she found wedging herself under the station wagon's steering wheel difficult to negotiate.

It was Thursday night. Bart had promised to come by after the deacon's meeting at the church. When he hadn't arrived by midnight, she became concerned. It'd been a long day and she was tired. If Bart wasn't going to make it, she needed to get to bed.

When he still hadn't arrived at 12:15, she decided to step out onto the porch, to see if she could see his flashlight moving along the creek. In the dim glow of the moon, she mistook a shadow for the porch's edge and tumbled down the steps, falling into a heap in the snow, her leg twisted beneath her. She lay helpless, unable to move. Although she struggled to pull herself to the steps, the excruciating pain in her leg and her oversized body wouldn't allow it.

The howling of the wind and the noise from the television she'd left turned on muffled her screams and no one heard her cries for help. Exhausted, she turned to the One who *could* hear her. "Lord, please! Send someone to help. Or let Kerel or Kari hear me. And, Lord, please. I beg of You. Don't let anything have happened to my baby!"

eleven

Tears rolled down Trish's cheeks as the pain in her leg increased. And she was cold, so cold, as the fluffy snow enveloped her traumatized body. Within minutes, she saw it. Bart's flashlight moving along the creek, heading toward her, and she thanked God for answered prayer.

Her heart pounded furiously as she lay there, watching as he grew nearer and nearer, until he was close enough to hear her as she cried out, "Bart! Help!"

His rhythmic footsteps turned into a run as he propelled himself toward the sound of her voice.

"Trish? Where are you?"

The beam from his flashlight crisscrossed over the new-fallen snow as he moved in the direction of the cabin.

"Here! At the foot of the steps! I fell!"

His run broke into a full sprint and soon he was kneeling beside her. "Trish! You don't even have a coat! You must be frozen!"

"It's my leg. I think it's broken!" she cried out as she reached toward him.

Within moments he'd securely splinted her leg and wrapped her in a blanket. He then scooped her up into the warmth of his arms, being careful to move her leg no more than necessary, and carried her into the house, closing the door and shutting out the cold behind him. "What were you doing outside?"

"Looking for you," she said shyly, trying to ignore the pain coursing through her body.

"Oh, Trish." He lowered her gently onto the sofa and

placed a pillow beneath her leg. "I've got to get you to the hospital. That leg needs attention." He pointed at her hairline. "You must've hit your head. You're bleeding!"

She lifted her fingertips and touched her forehead. It hurt. Between feeling so cold and the pain in her leg, she hadn't noticed it before. "I guess I did. It all happened so fast. How could I have been so careless?" She began to weep softly. "I might have hurt my baby, Bart."

He wrapped her in his arms and kissed her tear-stained cheeks. "The baby is okay, I know it. God has brought you this far, and He's still here for you now. Don't worry."

His reassurance was comforting, and she began to relax against the warmth of his strong body. "Thanks, Bart. You always make things seem better. I'm so glad you're here."

"I'm going to wake Kerel up and tell her I'm taking you to the hospital." He removed the damp blanket and took the patchwork quilt she'd been working on and placed it over her chilled body. "Try to relax, okay?"

They decided it would save time if they drove the old station wagon rather than wait until Bart could retrace his steps to his pickup. He backed it as close to the house as he could, warmed it up, and carried her to the backseat as easily as if she were a rag doll. Once she was settled, her splinted leg supported by pillows, they headed down the long driveway toward the hospital.

The emergency room was busy, but they took Trish in immediately. Bart stayed in the crowded waiting room, wringing his hands, while they wheeled Trish to radiology.

When she returned the doctor confirmed their amateur diagnosis. "Well, as far as I can tell, your baby appears to be fine, but it might be a good idea have your regular doctor check you out tomorrow, just to make sure. Unfortunately, your leg is broken. It's not a bad break, but you'll have to keep off of it. We'll put a soft cast on you for now. In two weeks, if your bones are knitting properly, we'll give you a walking cast and you can use a walker to get around."

"How long before I can stand on it?" Trish asked fearfully. "Without the cast or the walker?"

"Probably about six weeks."

She cast a glance at Bart who seemed to be taking the news as badly as she was.

"It's important that you stay off of that leg, Mrs. Taylor. Especially in your condition," the doctor stated emphatically as he eyed her protruding stomach. "You could do irreparable damage. Right now, the bones are aligned, but if you don't keep off of it, it could mean surgery."

"She'll stay off of it. I'll see to that," Bart assured him. "What about that cut on her head?"

"It's nothing to worry about. Just a surface wound, but it'll need a couple small stitches."

Trish reached for Bart's hand. "Stitches? I've never had stitches."

"It'll hurt a little, but you'll do fine," the doctor explained as he bent for a better look at the cut. "Once we get that stitched up, I'd like to keep you overnight to make sure you don't have any other injuries we aren't aware of yet."

"I can't!"

"Oh, yes, you can," Bart corrected. "I'll drive back and get Hildy to stay with the girls and get them off to school in the morning."

"But what about Zana?" she asked as the back of her hand brushed across her eyes.

"If Hildy can't take her up to the house, I'll pick her up before the girls leave for school. Don't you worry about a thing. Just do what the doctor says."

"I'll need to have you fill out some insurance papers so we can get you admitted," the doctor said matter-of-factly.

"I don't—"

"I'll cover her costs."

"Fine. Just tell the nurse."

Trish put her hand on Bart's arm. "You can't."

"Who says? You?" he quipped with a grin. "You're in no condition to argue with me. Of course I'll cover the costs. Isn't that what friends are for? To be there when you need them?"

The doctor turned to Bart. "Sounds like you have your work cut out for you. She'll be fine. As soon as we get that head stitched up and her leg taken care of, we'll get her tucked into a bed. She should have a fairly restful night. You can pick her up tomorrow."

"I'll be here in the morning," Bart promised. "Early in the morning."

"Oh, Bart. What have I done? Just when things seemed to be settling down." Trish tightened her grip on his hand, wishing he could stay with her all night.

He bent and kissed her cheek. "Don't worry. I'll take care of everything, Dandelion."

She watched him go. Once again, Bart Ryan had come to her rescue.

❧

Bart drove Trish's old station wagon down the lane toward the caretaker's cabin with the headlights turned off. Good thing he had a clearance card for the gate, otherwise he would have had to press the intercom to gain entrance to the Grayson grounds. He parked near the hedge behind the house and made his way warily to the little apartment above the garage, where he rapped on the window. Within seconds, a woman's round face appeared and she motioned him to the door.

"What's wrong, Bart? Why are you here?"

"Bad news, Hildy. Trish fell down the steps and broke her leg. And she cut her head bad enough to require stitches, but the baby is okay as far as we know."

She blinked and rubbed her eyes. "How did you know? I didn't even think you knew Trish."

"It's a long story. Trish can tell you later. Right now, I have to know if you can stay with the girls the rest of the night and get them off to school in the morning. The doctor insisted on keeping her overnight—"

"She's in the hospital?"

He nodded. "Yes. Can you take keep Zana with you tomorrow? Until they release Trish?"

Hildy nodded her head. "Yes, of course. Tell Trish not to worry. I'll watch after all three girls 'til she gets home." She frowned. "Or will you be seeing Trish?"

"Yes. I'm going to the hospital in the morning. I'll be bringing her home. She'd going to need both of us for the next few weeks."

"I'll help in any way I can. You tell her that. We'll manage somehow."

"Well, I'll do all I can, too. Thanks, Hildy. I knew she could count on you. I'm going to the cabin now. Do you want to come with me?"

Hildy gathered the few things she'd need, slipped into her coat, and accompanied Bart to the car, holding fast to his arm as they plodded through the heavy snow toward the driveway.

"I know you have questions, and you deserve answers, Hildy. I'd prefer Trish explain, okay?"

Hildy nodded as she climbed into the old station wagon.

⁂

"Hi," Bart said cheerily as he thrust a bouquet of fresh cut flowers into Trish's hand the next morning. "How are you? Did you sleep well? Has the doctor been in?"

"I'm doing fine." Trish took the flowers and sniffed at their sweet fragrance. "Oh, Bart, you shouldn't have. But thank you, I love them." She motioned to the chair beside her bed.

"Dr. Hancock was here."

"He wasn't worried about the baby, was he?"

She patted his hand reassuringly. "No. He examined me and said the baby took my fall in stride."

He let out a low whistle. "The way that boy kicks, he's got to be a tough little guy."

"Bart! You don't know this baby is a boy!"

"Whether it's a boy or a girl, that baby's mother better not be moving that leg any more than necessary for the next two weeks or she'll be going to the delivery room in a wheelchair," the resident doctor warned as he entered the room with her release papers. "I'll get the nurse to bring a wheelchair and you can go home."

They watched the man leave. As soon as Bart was sure he was out of sight, he bent over Trish and kissed her fully on her lips. "You're beautiful."

"Fat, and in this ridiculous hospital gown, with no makeup and my hair uncombed? Bart! You really know how to lift a girl's spirits. Let's go home."

≈

Once Bart had Trish settled on the sofa in the caretaker's cabin, he walked to the house to see Hildy and fetch little Zana.

"Mrs. Grayson knows," the cook whispered as she opened the door. "I had to tell her. She found Zana in the upstairs bedroom."

"Does she know I'm the one who took her to the hospital?"

Hildy shook her head. "She didn't ask and probably assumes she went in an ambulance or a taxi. I didn't tell her any different."

"Good."

For the next two weeks, Hildy delivered Trish's lunch to the cabin and packed the girls' lunch boxes. Bart furnished the family's supper, bringing it by on his way home from work, being careful to avoid observation by those in Grayson House.

Soon Trish was ready to start using the walker. She hadn't seen either of her parents—only Hildy and Bart.

"Here, let me put my arm around you," Bart cautioned the first time she tried to stand in the walking cast. "We can't have you taking another fall."

She took a deep breath and stood, with Bart's help, her hands tightly clutching the walker's handles. When a knock sounded on the door, Trish moved to open it, with Bart watching apprehensively.

"Hello, Mrs. Taylor," Detective Mercer said as he removed his hat and stepped inside.

"You know Bart Ryan, Detective Mercer?" Trish asked, a bit shaken by having someone find Bart in her cabin.

The detective extended his hand. "Yes, I know Mr. Ryan." Turning to Trish, he said, "The cook told me you broke your leg."

She nodded. "Yes, but it's healing just fine."

"I wanted you to take a look at these pictures and to see if any of these men look familiar to you."

Trish lowered herself onto the sofa with Bart's assistance as the detective spread the photos on the coffee table.

"Look at them one at a time."

Trish picked up the first photo. She'd never seen the man before. Nor the man in the second photo. But as she picked up the third one, she gasped.

"You recognize him?" the detective asked.

Bart moved in for a better look. "Well, what do you know."

twelve

"It's the man in the restaurant!" Trish shouted as her hand went to her mouth.

"What restaurant?" the detective quizzed, obviously pleased to have the suspect identified.

"A Denver steak house!" Trish held the photo in her hands, staring at it.

"You're sure you've seen him before?"

"Oh, yes. I remember him very well," she conceded.

Detective Mercer took the photo from her hand. "When was this?"

"Several months ago."

"What made you remember him? His clothes? Loud voice? Maybe he caused a ruckus in the restaurant?"

Trish weighed her words carefully, knowing she had no choice but to explain. "Yes, sorta." She looked to Bart for help.

"I drove Trish to Denver for her doctor's appointment, and we ate at that restaurant. That's where we saw him," he explained.

"Was he alone or with someone?"

Trish let loose a big sigh and rubbed her hands over her face. "With someone."

"Would you recognize the other person?"

"Yes," she admitted.

"Someone you knew?"

"Yes."

"Well, who?" the detective asked, obviously intrigued.

Trish gulped. "My mother. Olivia Grayson."

Detective Mercer sat up straight, his brows lifted in surprise. "Olivia Grayson is your mother?"

She nodded. "Yes, she is."

"And no one thought to mention that fact to me before now," he said suspiciously. "And the man was with your mother? Did she introduce you to him? Do you know his name?"

"No, she didn't. She didn't know we were in the restaurant. She didn't see us. We—uh, didn't want to—interrupt."

"Could you hear their conversation?"

"No, they were too far away."

He leaned toward her. "I know this is hard for you, Mrs. Taylor, but you must tell me everything you can." He took his pad from his pocket and hurriedly began writing notes. "This man may be a suspect in the burglary."

After a sideways glance toward Bart, she related the happenings between her mother and the man, including the way Olivia had slapped him. "Do you really think he could have anything to do with my mother's missing jewelry?"

"We'll know more when we've had a chance to interrogate him." He backed toward the door. "I appreciate your cooperation. You'll be hearing from me. Meantime, take care of that leg."

"I was just leaving, too." Bart buttoned his jacket, told Trish good-bye, and followed the man, closing the door behind him.

She leaned back into the sofa. *Oh, Mother. What have you done?*

In less than two hours, Trish heard footsteps on the porch and the door opened. There stood her mother, wrapped from head to toe in fur, with an angry scowl on her face, the heavy fragrance of her perfume wafting into the room. "I hope you're happy, young lady. Lying to that detective like you did!"

"I didn't lie, Mother. I told him exactly what I saw. You

and that man having an argument in that steak house in Denver. I saw you slap him. Hard!"

Olivia bent over her daughter, towering menacingly above her. "Well, you were wrong, Patricia. It certainly wasn't me!"

Trish looked her straight in the eye. "It was you, Mother, without a doubt. Bart saw you, too."

"Bart? The man who does our gardening? He was there?" Her mother was livid.

"Yes. He drove me to the doctor in Denver. Then we had lunch in that restaurant. We both saw you there with that man."

"You'll be sorry for this, Patricia. When you find out I wasn't even there, you'd better be prepared to apologize!" She rushed through the still-open door, slamming it hard behind her.

When Bart returned late that night, the two of them tried to unravel the mystery surrounding her mother. None of it made any sense.

❧

Two days before Christmas, Bart arrived with his boys and a Christmas tree, complete with decorations and lights. After trimming it, the two families ate pizza and sang Christmas carols. Bart and Trish sat on the sofa and watched as their children teased one another.

"They sure get along well, don't they?" Bart asked as he carefully lifted her leg onto the footstool.

"Yes," she answered with a smile. "But, Bart, I'm worried. I haven't heard a thing about the burglary since Detective Mercer and my mother came to the house. It's eerie. I thought for sure my father would come pounding on my door, ordering me to leave."

Bart frowned. "Maybe your mother never told him. Maybe she didn't want him to know about us identifying the man. The only way she could tell him about us was to tell him about that guy."

"Hmm. You may be right."

He grinned as he took her hand. "Whatever the reason, I'm just glad I've been able to spend time with you while you've been convalescing with that leg. Now, tell me what you want for Christmas."

"You. You, and the boys. Right here for Christmas dinner with the girls and me. With the help of the walker, I think I can put a decent meal together. That's the best present I could ask for."

"You got it. We'll be here."

❧

The delicious aroma of baked chicken and dressing, creamy mashed potatoes, pumpkin pie, and homemade rolls greeted Bart and his three sons when they arrived at the cabin Christmas Day.

"Umm, can we have dessert first?" Bart begged as he eyed the warm pies resting on the trivets.

"You overgrown child! If you finish your veggies, you can have pie. Not a minute sooner," she told him with a giggle.

After consuming the great meal she'd prepared, with Kerel's and Kari's help, the Taylors and the Ryans gathered around the Christmas tree as Bart opened his Bible and read the Christmas story from the second chapter of Luke.

"I love the baby Jesus," Zana said as she sat on Zeb's lap, twirling her fingers through his hair.

"We all love the baby Jesus," Bart declared, closing the Bible. "He was God's only Son. Do you know why He sent His only Son to earth?"

"To die on the cross," Andy said sadly. "I wish He didn't have to die."

"Me, either," Zana added with a puckered up face.

"He had to die. It was God's plan," Kyle explained.

"To save us from our sins," Andy spoke up from his place beside the footstool.

Bart beamed with pride. "Yes, you're all right. Think how

much it hurt God to see His Son treated so badly. God knew His Son would die on the cross. Even when Jesus was a baby, He knew His Son would have to die for the sins of the world. But Jesus didn't die in vain. You know what?"

Zana turned to him, her eyes now sparkling. "Uh-huh. He rosed again. He lives!"

"You're right, honey. Jesus lives. That's why we don't fear what tomorrow brings. God loves us, and He cares for us. Don't you think we should thank Him for all He does?"

They held hands, forming a circle, and bowed their heads in prayer. Bart led off, with Zeb next, then Kerel, and finally, Trish.

"How about next year? Wanna do this again?" Bart asked their hostess as their families said good night.

"Dreamer!" She gave him a quick peck on the cheek.

"That was a great dinner. You get around pretty good for a fat girl on crutches," he teased as he gave her a gentle pat on her abdomen. "Doesn't she, little boy?"

"Bart!"

He grinned sheepishly as he gave her hand an affectionate squeeze and backed out the door. "Take care of that little man."

"Merry Christmas, Bart."

"Merry Christmas, Trish."

≈

"You don't have long to wait, Mrs. Taylor." Dr. Hancock wrapped the cuff around her arm and prepared to take her blood pressure. "Getting anxious?"

She flinched as the cuff tightened. "Very!"

"Well, let's hope this baby holds off until you get that cast off. How much longer do you have to wear that thing?"

"Two weeks."

"Let's make your appointment for one week this time. We want to keep a close eye on that baby of yours."

The phone was ringing when Trish unlocked the door.

It was Detective Mercer.

"I need you to come down to the station and make an identification. We've made an arrest."

"You caught the man?" she asked in surprise.

"Yes. We're sure we have the right man; we just have to prove it."

"The man. . .with my mother?" she asked cautiously, hoping for her mother's sake he'd say no.

"We'll discuss that when you come down here. Would you like me to send a car for you?"

"No. I'll get there myself. Thank you."

As soon as she hung up the phone she called Bart, who agreed he should drive her to the police station.

❧

"Take your time. There'll be several people in the lineup. Look at them one at a time. Point out the man you saw meeting with your mother, only if you are sure it's him. Okay?"

Detective Mercer led her into a small room and asked her to be seated. When the group of men appeared behind the glass, she recognized the man immediately and pointed him out to the detective.

"You're sure?" he asked.

"Absolutely. Now what?"

"Next we'll have Mr. Ryan see if he can identify the man and we'll go from there."

He took her by the arm and helped her manipulate the walker through the narrow doorway.

"You're sure he's the one who took my mother's jewelry?"

"That's for a judge to decide. It's our job to gather the evidence."

❧

Trish leaned her head against the seat of Bart's SUV wearily. Walking long distances with the excess weight of the baby, even with the walker, tired her quickly. "Do you think my mother suspected that man took her jewelry?"

He shrugged his shoulders as he wove through traffic. "Beats me. Seems she knew him pretty well in the restaurant that day. What do you think?"

"I don't know. But I do know one thing. If she did, my father is going to be furious!"

Her father summoned Trish to the house the next morning. "I suppose you've heard what has happened."

She winced. "I'm not sure what you're taking about."

He motioned toward the chair. "Sit down, Patricia."

She thumped the walker across the floor and seated herself.

Wilmer ran his hand over his face with a deep sigh. "The police have arrested the man who pawned your mother's jewelry. Apparently, it was the man you saw with your mother in a restaurant in Denver several months ago."

"That man came into this house and stole her jewelry?" Trish was unable to imagine such thing.

Her father's face formed a deep scowl. "Not exactly. It seems your mother gave him the jewelry."

"What?" she shouted with surprise. "She gave him her jewelry? Why?"

"That's what I'm trying to find out. I'd thought perhaps you knew why she'd do such a ridiculous thing. Maybe you'd overheard their conversation that day. So far, your mother won't tell me why, and it appears she is in trouble because of you, Patricia. I hope you're proud of yourself!"

"Me? I only told the detective the truth—that I'd seen the two of them together."

"That information was none of your concern. You should have kept it to yourself."

"But—"

"You'd do well to mind your own business, young lady. Don't you have enough to do without prying into the lives of others? By the way, when is that due?" he asked as his gaze went to her abdomen.

She stiffened. "That—is a baby, and it could come most anytime within the next two weeks."

"Then that means you'll be moving out soon. You've caused enough trouble in this family already. Now this. Your poor mother is a bundle of nerves. And you're responsible—after all she's done for you."

Trish's jaw dropped. "What I've done? How can you say that, Father? Are you putting me out as soon as my baby is born?"

"You've cast suspicion on your mother, that's what! Your own mother. And yes, I want you out of here. If it weren't for her, I would never have allowed you stay in the first place. It was her idea for you to move into the caretaker's cabin. But that was before we found out that you were pregnant again."

"I didn't kn—"

"I've heard enough of your lies, Patricia. Go on welfare if you must. We've lived through one of your fiascoes; we can make it through another if we have to. I'm sure people will understand our actions when they learn how you've treated us."

Trish couldn't believe her ears. How could he be so blind? She stood to her feet, her hands grasping the walker as she glared at him with her chin held high. "I'll be out of here and out of your lives as soon as I possibly can!"

Wilmer seemed surprised at her resolve, as if he'd expected her to grovel at his feet. "I'll give you a thousand dollars when you're ready to leave," he offered. "That should carry you for few weeks, until you can get a job."

"I'll take that thousand dollars for my children's sake. But I intend to pay it back. Every dollar. I still have my pride. That's one thing you can't take away from me." Shoving the walker in front of her for support, she hurried from the room.

❧

"He actually told you to move out?" Bart asked as he sat in the caretaker's cabin late that night, long after the children had gone to bed. "How could he do that to his own daughter? I don't get it!"

"Me, either. Father and I have never been close, but I never doubted he loved me, in his own inhibited way."

"Old Wilmer has to be crazy not to love you, Trish. And those beautiful girls of yours. He's gotta have a screw loose."

She laughed. "You really think so?"

"I know so. And I'm pretty smart," he joked as he pulled her close to him.

"Not smart enough to stay away from me," she chided with a jab of her elbow to his side. "If my dad is this cruel to his daughter, can you imagine what he'll do to you when he finds out you were at that restaurant with me?"

"Let him. I'm tired of sneaking around. If it weren't for what he could do to you, I'd have—"

She pressed her finger to his lips. "Shh! Let's hope he never finds out."

"Well, you can count on me. I'd never let you down."

"I know, Bart. But I hope I never have to come to you for a handout. Like I told my father, I have my pride," she said with a tilt of her chin.

"I say, let's change the subject. I want to know how that little guy is taking all of this. Still trying to kick his way outta there?"

She took his hand and carefully placed it on the rise of her abdomen. "What do you think?"

Bart's eyes widened. "That kid is really kickin'. Does he do that all night, too?"

"Bart," she said correcting him with a playful frown. "That *he* may very well be a *she!*"

"And *he* may very well be a *he!*"

She leaned her head against his shoulder with a girlish giggle. "You're incorrigible!"

He loved to hear her laugh. No matter what was going on

in her life, she could laugh. And like the Scripture said, "A cheerful heart is good medicine." One thing of which he was certain—whatever happened to Patricia Taylor, she'd end up on her feet.

᠉

Trish had a restless night. When she finally crawled out of bed at six, she felt like she'd been wrestling with tigers.

Her morning didn't go much better. From time to time, her abdominal muscles would cramp and she'd double over, laying the blame on the late-night bowl of ice cream she'd had with Bart.

By noon the cramps had turned to frequent pangs of dull pain and she knew she was beginning labor. By the time the girls got home from school, her pains were coming regularly enough she could time them.

By six o'clock, she knew she'd better take action. Her pains were getting closer and closer together. After a loving kiss and hug, and a reminder of how much she loved them, her three daughters were sent to Hildy. As she crossed the room to call the taxi, the phone rang.

"How's that boy doing?" a familiar voice asked.

"Bart, how many times do I have to remind you this baby may be—*aagh!*" She gasped as an immobilizing contraction caused her to double over.

"Trish! What is it? Are you okay?" he asked with alarm.

With her hand pressed firmly across her abdomen and her eyes clamped tightly shut, she held her breath and waited until the pain subsided before answering. "I'm in labor! I have to call a taxi!"

"Trish. Hang on. I'm only a few blocks from you. I'm on my way! Don't call a taxi!"

"No, Bart. You're too involved already. A taxi will be—*aaagh*—fine. I'm sure I have time before the baby arrives. Don't come!"

"I am coming! Stay on the phone with me. Okay?"

He arrived in a matter of minutes, driving his pickup right up to the cabin porch. "You okay?" he asked as he rushed in through the door.

"I'm fine. But you should've let me call—*aagh!*" She grabbed the chair's back for support as another pain, more severe than the last, doubled her body in half.

Bart grabbed her suitcase with one hand and her arm with the other. "I'm getting you to the hospital! Come on!"

&

"She's in labor," Bart shouted as they entered the ER.

Within minutes, Trish had been checked in, dressed in a hospital gown, and attached to monitors. Soon, Dr. Hancock appeared, much to the anxious couple's relief.

"Umm. I've never delivered a baby to a mother wearing a cast on her leg. Thought you were going to get rid of that thing, Trish," the doctor chided with a chuckle as he thumped on the cast.

"I was supposed to get if off tomorrow, but my plans were altered slightly," she mused as her hands clenched the bed rails in preparation for the pain she felt revving up deep within her.

"Well, that leg is going to have to wait. It looks like our baby is ready to make its entrance into the world. You ready, Trish?"

She nodded. "Am I!"

"She gonna be okay, Doc?"

"Bart! She's gonna have a baby, not brain surgery," Dr. Hancock quipped as he watched the wiggly lines on the monitor. "Relax!"

"Bart brought me to the hospital, Dr. Hancock. I think he was afraid he'd have to deliver this baby himself," Trish added with a gasp as the next pain hit her with a vengeance.

Dr. Hancock watched the monitor until the pain subsided. "Bart, it's time for you to go to the waiting room. This baby is getting down to business. We'll let you know as soon as it arrives."

Trish watched as Bart turned to leave. "Bart!" She extended her hand to him. "Would you pray for us before you go?"

"Sure," he answered with a big smile as he took her hand in his and knelt beside her bed.

It was the sweetest prayer she'd ever heard as he asked God to protect her and give her a safe delivery. Her body seemed to absorb a renewed strength as he prayed, her hands cupped in his. When he said, "Amen," he kissed her fingers. "I'll be in the waiting room, praying for you. You're not alone, Trish."

"I know. Thank you, Bart." She winced as another pain seized her body. This one, the hardest of them all.

ঙ

An hour later, Dr. Hancock tapped Bart on the shoulder. "Your prayers did the trick. She's fine. And so is the baby."

Bart rose to his feet and shook the man's hand vigorously. "What was it, Doc? A boy or girl?"

thirteen

Dr. Hancock gave him a wry grin. "Maybe you'd better ask Trish. She's asking for you."

"I can go see her?"

"Sure. She and that baby of hers breezed through the delivery. She's a plucky little gal."

Bart grinned as he followed the doctor to the birthing room where Trish lay in the bed with a bundle of joy tucked in her arm and a smile a yard wide on her weary face. God *had* answered his prayer. Other than looking a little spent, she was as beautiful as ever. "So?" he asked as he bent to kiss her cheek. "Boy or girl?"

She pulled back the fluffy white blanket from the baby's pink face. "You were right, Mr. Know-it-all."

Bart leaned in close "I knew it. Look at those fists. That kid is a boy, all right. Whatcha gonna name him?"

"Jake, maybe? After his father?"

"I think that would be a fine name for this little man." He slipped his little finger into the baby's clenched fist. "Look, Trish. Look how he's holding on to my finger. What a strong little guy he is. Wait'll his sisters see him. They're gonna love him."

"Bart. Thank you," she said, her face growing serious. "For being here with me. You don't know how much it means to me. I was so afraid I'd have to go through this alone. You're a very special man."

"And you're a very special woman, my little dandelion. You've survived again!"

"Would you do me another favor?"

"Of course, just name it!"

"Would you go tell my girls they have a little brother?"

❧

Trish lay in the semidarkness of the hospital room, thankful for the uncomplicated birth of her new baby, yet, at the same time, questioning the future of her little family. Now that little Jake Taylor had arrived, she was being forced to move on with her life.

❧

"We're home!" Trish called out as Bart pushed open the door to the caretaker's cabin.

Three exuberant girls rushed to meet their new brother as Bart stood proudly by, suitcase in hand.

"He's so cute," Kari said as she pulled the cover from the baby's little round face.

"Oh, Mama. He's got so much hair!" Kerel added as she touched the baby fluff with her hand.

"I love him," little Zana said as she planted a sticky kiss on the baby's forehead. "Can we keep him?"

Bart laughed and lifted the little girl up into his arms. "Sure you can keep him, honey. He's not a puppy!"

"Might as well be," Trish said with a tinge of sarcasm. "Our little family is being turned out like a litter of unwanted puppies."

"Don't worry, dandelion. God is faithful, He'd never let you down and neither will I."

"I know. I'm counting on you both," she answered with a smile.

"Well, you need to rest. You and that baby. I'm going to leave now, but I'll be back tonight with supper."

The next four days were happy ones for the little family. Hildy delivered their lunches and Bart brought in supper. The baby was doing fine and Trish's heart was overflowing with love. The doctor gave her permission to remove the cast from her leg, and with the support of a cane she was able to get around on it quite nicely.

She scanned the papers daily, in search of both a small house to rent and a job. She wondered how many days her father would allow her to stay now that the baby was here. A week? Two weeks?

Eager to share her good news about little Jake's birth, she phoned the pastor of the church she and Jake had attended in Wichita. He and his wife had been so good to her when her husband died so suddenly.

When she confided in him about her financial situation and her need to find a house for her family, as well as a job, he said, "Come back to Wichita, Trish. Remember the little house next door to the parsonage? We're going to wreck it next fall to extend the parking lot. You can live in it until then, rent free! And one of the ladies in the church's day care center is quitting. You can take her job. Doesn't pay much, but you won't have to hire a sitter while you work."

When a knock sounded on her door, she was surprised to find, not Bart, whom she'd expected, but her mother, Hildy, and Detective Mercer, standing side by side on her porch, and none of them looked happy.

"Mrs. Taylor. We have something to tell you. I'd suggest you let Hildy take the girls up to the house with her. You may not want them to hear what we have to say."

Trish looked to her mother for approval and was surprised when she nodded her consent.

"Please sit down, Mrs. Taylor," the detective suggested after Hildy had taken the girls to the main house. He motioned both Trish and her mother toward the sofa.

Trish could read terror in her mother's eyes and it frightened her.

"I'll get right to the point. We've arrested a man in

connection with the theft of your mother's jewelry. You saw that man and your mother together in a restaurant in Denver."

Trish shot a glance toward her mother who was sitting with her hands folded in her lap, her head hung low.

"Your mother said she always kept her jewelry locked in the safe and no one but her, your father, and your sister knew the combination. Yet, the jewelry was stolen." He stood and began to pace the floor as he spoke.

"Other than your information, we had no leads. We were at a dead end until the jewelry turned up at three different pawnshops in the Denver area. The pawnbrokers looked at our mug books and all three identified the same man."

Trish stiffened. "The man I identified?"

He stopped his pacing and nodded. "Yes. The same man. He wasn't difficult to find. Guys like him rarely are. Anyway, once he realized he'd been identified, he decided he'd do anything to save his neck, so he gave us the name of his accomplice."

Trish's hand went to her mouth. "Who was it?"

He turned to Olivia. "Do you want to tell her, or should I?"

Olivia shook her head and said nothing.

"Very well, I'll tell her. His accomplice was your mother. She gave him her jewelry."

"But why? Why would you do that, Mother? And how did you know that awful man?" Trish asked, shocked by his statement. How could this be happening? None of it made any sense. Her mother helped that man?

"She's known the man for many years, long before you were born. She gave him the jewelry so he could pawn it to get the cash he needed, then claimed it'd been stolen from the safe."

"But. . . Why?"

"I think your mother ought to answer that one."

Trish leaned toward Olivia and looked into her sad eyes. She'd never seen her overconfident mother like this, and she felt sorry for her. "Mother? Why?"

Olivia's trembling fingers clamped over her daughter's hand. "This is so hard for me."

"I know it's hard, Mrs. Grayson. But your daughter has to be told," the detective warned.

"He needed money, Trish. So he came to me and threatened me. It was impossible to get my hands on that much cash—without your father knowing. Then we came up with the idea of claiming the jewelry had been stolen."

"But," Trish interjected, "it happened twice!"

Olivia swallowed hard and cleared her throat before going on. "I thought he'd be happy with the money he got from pawning my diamond ring and emerald necklace. But he wasn't. He came back for more, and I had to give it to him."

"Why, Mother? I don't understand."

"He was blackmailing her, Mrs. Taylor," the detective interjected. "If he hadn't been caught, he would've wanted more and more."

"I know that now." Her mother lowered her chin with an air of defeat. "I was stupid to think I could trust him."

"But, Mother. Blackmail? What could he possibly blackmail you with?"

"Tell her, Mrs. Grayson," he admonished.

"I—ah—he. . ." Tears filled Olivia's eyes and tumbled down her cheeks as she turned to her daughter. "He–he's your father, Patricia."

The room began to spin, lights flashed, and her vision became blurry. Trish felt herself whirling backward into a long, dark tunnel. It was nearly impossible to zero in on the words they were saying.

"Patricia! Patricia! Try to sit up and take a drink of water," her mother was pleading. "Please, Patricia, please."

Slowly the room came into focus and she was able, with the help of Detective Mercer, to sit up and lean her head against the sofa's soft back.

"What happened?"

"Take another drink. You fainted," he explained gently as he took the glass from Olivia's shaking fingers and offered it to her daughter. "You've had quite a shock."

Then she remembered. She remembered why her mother and the detective were in her home. She remembered Olivia's admission and looked searchingly into her mother's troubled face. "The—the man in the restaurant?"

"Yes," Olivia replied softly as she stroked her eldest daughter's cheek. "He's your father."

Trish blinked hard to clear her head. "You're telling me that man's my father? I don't understand."

Olivia took a deep breath and let it out slowly. "I'm sure you want to hear the whole ugly story." She rose to her feet, crossed the room, and seated herself in an empty chair, as if needing to put space between herself and the daughter she'd deceived since birth.

Trish simply stared at her, still in shock from her mother's startling announcement.

Olivia fumbled in her purse for a tissue and blotted her eyes before continuing. "I—ah—married Wilmer when I was quite young. I'll be honest with you, Patricia. I didn't love him, not like you said you loved Jake. I wanted the money and position he represented, so when he asked me to marry him, I said yes. Then, well. . . I became bored with him and his way of life very quickly. We had nothing in common. He wanted to work, I wanted to party. He wanted to make money, I—I wanted to spend it. He wanted to socialize with people his age. I wanted to hang out with the younger crowd. Eventually," she said, avoiding her daughter's penetrating gaze, "I met Bill and he swept me off my feet. He was lively and fun, had a wonderful personality, and was a great dancer. He paid attention to me, treated me like a queen, and showered me with gifts. And your father was so busy making money, he never even missed me."

She shifted her position. "I spent more and more time with Bill and next thing I knew—I was—pregnant. I thought he'd want to marry me. I was more than willing to leave Wilmer for him. But when I told Bill about you, he laughed in my face, said he wasn't ready to be a daddy." She shrugged her shoulders dejectedly.

"He left town and I never saw him again, until late last summer, when he called me and asked for money. He said if I didn't give it to him, he'd tell Wilmer about our affair, and about you, and he'd tell the newspapers, too. I had no choice but to give him what he wanted." She hung her head in shame.

"So, I'm not Fa—Wilmer's daughter? Does he know?"

Olivia shook her head. "No, you're not. And so far, Wilmer doesn't know any differently. He thinks you're his."

Detective Mercer added, "She's hoping he won't have to be told, but we can't make any promises. At this point I don't see any way the truth can be kept from Mr. Grayson. I've recommended that Mrs. Grayson tell him herself. But that decision is up to her."

"I–I—ah." Olivia seemed to choke on her words. "I'm sorry, Patricia. I didn't think this would ever come out."

You may be sure that your sins will find you out, Trish thought as she stared at her distraught mother. "And you had the nerve to demand I have an abortion when I was pregnant with Jake's baby all those years ago? How could you? Knowing what you'd done? You were so high-and-mighty. You treated me like I was the lowest of the low."

Olivia buried her face in her hands and wept openly. "I was

so young, and they didn't perform abortions so easily then. I decided having you and pretending you were Wilmer's child was the best thing for everyone."

"But why did you treat me so badly? Why didn't you stand up to Father—him—in my behalf? I was your daughter!"

Her mother lifted watery eyes, her cheeks stained with mascara. "I don't know. I just don't know. I guess I was afraid to go against your father's wishes. He was so determined to break you and Jake up. He was sure you'd come running back home and do away with that baby. He never expected you to get married. He never believed your threats."

"Now what?" Trish asked the detective. "Where do we go from here?"

"The ball is in your mother's court for the moment. It's her decision." He motioned to Olivia. "We'd better be going now. Mr. Grayson will be coming home soon."

"I really am sorry, Patricia," Olivia offered as she followed the officer's lead and the door closed behind them.

Trish carefully dropped to her knees beside the sofa and poured out her heart to God, her heavenly Father.

❧

"That man is your father?" Bart flung his arms about Trish and buried his face in her hair.

She'd told him the whole story as soon as he'd arrived, every sordid detail, just as Olivia had told it to her. "Wilmer Grayson is not my father. I still can't believe it."

"Now that I think about it, we shouldn't be so surprised. You're really nothing like him, you know."

Trish pulled a face. "I never was. He and I used to go round and round, locking horns constantly. I was always a disappointment to him. Ironic, isn't it? He disowned me all those years ago, and I wasn't even his daughter!"

"Wow, this sure puts your mother on the hot seat. What do you think she'll do? About telling him, I mean." Bart took little Jake from her arms and lowered himself into the new rocking chair he'd brought Trish as a present. "I'd sure hate to be in her shoes."

"That means Margaret is my half sister. No wonder she's more like my fath—Wilmer than I am."

"That old blood-is-thicker-than-water thing, huh?"

"Guess so," she agreed, her mood somber. "I hate to take his money, but that thousand dollars he offered me sure looks good. I'll need it to—"

"If you don't want to take his money, you can borrow it from me. Interest free. You could put this little boy up as collateral!" He slipped a finger beneath the baby's chubby chin.

"You!" She gave him an appreciative smile. "What would I do without you?"

Little Jake stirred in Bart's arms and then settled back into his deep sleep, his eyelids fluttering rapidly as if he were dreaming.

"Seriously, Bart, I've been thinking. Other than you and the boys, I have no ties to Cedar Ridge. I phoned my former pastor in Wichita last night, to tell him about the baby, and he offered to let me stay in the little house next door to the church, rent free, until they tear it down next fall to expand the parking lot. He even offered me a job in the church's day care center. It doesn't pay much, but I won't have to leave Jake or Zana with a sitter while I work."

Bart's eyes narrowed beneath a frown. "Go back to Wichita? You told him no thanks, didn't you?"

"I—ah, I told him I'd be there as soon as I could get things packed. I leave the day after tomorrow."

"Aw, Trish. Why'd you go and do that?" he asked in a voice loud enough to startle the sleeping baby.

"I'm living here on borrowed time, Bart. I have no other choice. Going back to Wichita is the best option I've got."

He frowned. "But what about us?"

She crossed the room and knelt by his chair, her hand on his wrist. "Bart, Dear. There is no *us!* You've been good to my family, and I've loved our time together. But let's face it. We each have children who are totally dependent upon us for their survival. You have three wonderful boys who adore you. I have three beautiful girls and a precious little boy that I intend to raise in the best way I can. You've lost Charlotte and I've lost Jake. You came into my life at a time when I needed you. You were an angel sent directly from God. Knowing you has given me a glimpse of what our heavenly Father is like. You are such a wonderful, godly man. But now it's time to move on with our lives."

His strong fingers cupped her hand. "No, Trish. You can't leave."

"I have to, Bart."

"I'll take care of you and the children. You don't have to go back to Wichita!"

"In the first place, you already have four mouths to feed. Taking on my family would bring that total to nine! Nine people, Bart! I couldn't ask you to do that. And, secondly, what do you think Wilmer would do if you took us in? He'd take the Grayson Industries account away from you in a heartbeat. Your dependents would more than double and your income would drop. That doesn't make good business sense. No, I won't even let you consider such a ridiculous thing."

She took the baby from his arms and placed him on the quilt in the little wooden box she'd prepared as his crib. "You'll always be the best friend I've ever had, and I'm grateful for all you've done, but my mind is made up. I made the decision last night, even before I learned I'm not Wilmer's daughter. I'm going to Wichita."

"We could get married."

"Married? How would that make things any different? You'd have just as many mouths to feed, and Wilmer would still cancel your contract. No! Thank you for your kind gesture, but answer me honestly. If I weren't in such trouble, would you be asking me to marry you?"

"Maybe not yet. . . ."

"That's what I thought. And, if I weren't in trouble, I wouldn't consider marriage to you at this time. Marriage shouldn't be a matter of convenience or obligation, Bart. It should be between two people who love each other and want to spend the rest of their lives together. And have children together."

"But I've already told you, I think I'm falling in love with you."

"But you're not sure, are you? Could it be we needed each other and we've mistaken that need for love? Could you really be happy binding yourself to a woman with four children? One of them a newborn?" Bart reached for her arm but she backed away. "You'd probably hate me in a year's time. Nine children, Bart? I think not. No. I have to go to Wichita."

"Trish—"

"Bart, please. Don't make this any harder than it already is. I have so much to do to get ready to go. We'd better say good-bye now."

"No, Trish. No," he pleaded to no avail.

She moved to the door and opened it slowly. "Please, Bart. Go home to your family."

His shoulders hunched in defeat as he moved past her and onto the porch, wringing his ball cap in his hands. "If you change your mind—"

"I won't. I can't," she murmured as she stood in the open doorway.

"Can I kiss you good-bye?" he asked shyly as he stepped forward.

She gave him a demure grin as her eyes filled with tears. "No. I'm afraid I might change my mind."

"I wouldn't complain about that," he answered with a tilt of his head.

"Please, Bart. I'll tell the children good-bye for you. And remember me to the boys."

"If you're sure—"

"I'm sure. Good-bye, Bart," she whispered as she closed the door on her best friend.

By the time the school bus pulled out the next morning, Trish was already at work loading the station wagon with her family's belongings. The phone rang several times, but she let the ancient answering machine record the messages. Most of the calls were from Bart. Each time, when she heard his voice pleading with her to pick up the phone, she nearly succumbed, her resolve wilting more with each ring.

She put her children to bed early, then packed up the few remaining items in the kitchen cabinet before retiring for the night, her last night in Cedar Ridge. The calls from Bart kept coming until way past midnight, and although it broke her heart, she didn't pick up the phone.

Turning her back on him was the hardest thing she'd ever had to do. As he walked out that door for the last time, she admitted to herself she loved him with all her heart. It was because of that love she had to let him go.

After breakfast the next morning, the Taylor family walked across the lawn to Grayson House to say their good-byes. Trish left her children with Hildy and Anna and went in search of her mother. As she entered the upstairs hallway, she heard a voice coming from Olivia's room. It was Wilmer's and he was angry.

"You thought you'd gotten away with it, didn't you, Olivia?" he shouted. "Well, let me tell you, you didn't! I knew about your lover, all about him. And I knew he was nothing but a loser. But you had to find that out for yourself, didn't you?"

"You knew?"

"I knew. I had you followed, Olivia, you and that no-good Bill. Did you really think you could pawn that illegitimate daughter of yours off on me as my child, and I wouldn't know it? How stupid did you think I was? I didn't get where I am today by being taken by foolish women!"

"But why?" Olivia asked. "If you knew, why did you stay married to me? Why did you accept Patricia as your child?"

Trish sobbed softly as she listened in the safety of the hall. No wonder the man had been so critical of her during her childhood. Each time he'd looked at her, he'd probably been reminded of her mother's infidelity.

His voice softened slightly. "Because I loved you. And I couldn't bring that kind of shame on the Grayson name. It would have killed my mother and father. But try as I may, I couldn't bring myself to love that baby of yours. I think she inherited her rebellious spirit from that man. It was obvious my blood wasn't flowing through her veins. Didn't you ever wonder why she and I never got along when she was growing up?"

"Of course I wondered," Olivia answered, her voice filled with anxiety. "I'm sure she did, too."

"When Patricia turned up pregnant with that boy's baby, it was like facing your betrayal all over again. And, like a bad penny, she turned up on our doorstep with those children of hers," he retorted.

"You're such a hard man, Wilmer," her mother remarked bitterly. "You won't have to put up with her much longer. Hildy said she's leaving today."

"Good riddance, I'd say."

Trish backed away quietly, her tears flowing unchecked,

her heart aching with the pain of rejection. The last thing on her mind was saying good-bye to her mother.

With a quick good-bye to Hildy and Anna, she loaded her family in the station wagon and drove away without so much as a backward look at Grayson House in the rearview mirror.

fourteen

Bart tried to concentrate on his work in the greenhouse but his mind kept wandering, remembering Trish's comment. *"Marriage shouldn't be a matter of convenience or obligation, Bart. It should be between two people who love each other and want to spend the rest of their lives together. And have children together."*

That was exactly what he wanted out of life. To love and be loved. To be a husband to Trish and a father to her children. To take care of her, love, and cherish her. Be one with her. And, if God willed, have children with her. He loved her! He'd loved her since that first day when she'd driven through the gate at Grayson House. How could he have been so stupid?

Bart tossed his trowel into the peat moss bin and peeled off his gardener's apron. *I love that woman and I'm going after her!* He hurried into the main building at Ryan Garden and Landscape and into the office area. *She's not going to Wichita if I can help it!*

His secretary looked up from her computer in surprise. "What are you doing, Bart? You look like a man with a mission!"

"I am! I'm leaving and I don't know when I'll be back. Anything comes up while I'm gone, take care of it, okay?" he ordered as he ran a comb though his unruly hair and slipped into his jacket. "Oh, and if I'm not back by three, drive to the school and pick up Andy and Kyle and take them to their grandmother's house. Ask her to keep 'em 'til Zeb gets home from track."

"But, Bart," the woman shouted as her boss moved out the

door like a whirlwind, "where are you going?"

"I'm gonna get me a wife!" he answered confidently with a big smile.

All the way to Grayson House, Bart rehearsed what he was going to say to Trish to convince her of his love. So what if he'd be taking on the added responsibility of a widow and her four children? So what if Wilmer Grayson chose to cancel his contract? Nothing really mattered except his love for Trish.

He prayed as his pickup wove in and out of traffic. *Lord, please. I love her so much. Give me the right words to say to convince her to stay, to become my wife. God, I realize now it was You who sent her to me and I praise You for her.*

Bart's heart sank as he hurried up the steps of the caretaker's cabin. It was quiet, too quiet. Trish and the children were gone.

He leaped back in the pickup and raced to Grayson House, hoping maybe, just maybe, Trish and the children were there, saying their good-byes.

Without taking time to ring the bell, he burst through the massive oak door and into the foyer where the angry face of Wilmer Grayson greeted him.

"Where's Trish?" he demanded, not taking time to mince words.

"How dare you come into my home like this! What do you want?" Wilmer shouted as he glared at his uninvited guest.

"Trish! Where is she?" Bart snapped back as his eyes scanned the big house.

"Gone," Olivia answered from somewhere behind him. "Hildy said she left about nine. She never even said good-bye."

Bart turned and glared at the woman. All he could think about was her deception about Trish's real father. "Where'd she go?"

"Maybe back to Wichita. I don't know," Olivia admitted as she moved to stand by her husband.

"Get out now," Wilmer ordered as he waved his cane through the air. "If your company wasn't doing such a good job, I'd fire you right now. Get out of here before I change my mind."

Bart stepped toward the man, wishing either he was a few years older or Wilmer was a few years younger, so he could punch him in the nose. "Well, Mr. Grayson, you can consider this as a cancellation notice. I don't want your business! I'm breaking our contract. Find yourself another company. Ryan Garden and Landscape is through with Grayson Industries, as of now!"

Wilmer looked as though he was about to explode as his face reddened and his eyes bulged in their sockets. "You can't—"

"I not only can—I just did!" With that, Bart pushed past the man, slamming the door behind him.

He checked his watch as he climbed into the pickup. If the Graysons were right, Trish had been on the road to Wichita for a little over an hour. Undoubtedly, she'd drive Interstate 70 from Denver to Salina, Kansas, then take Highway 81 into Wichita. But with four children and no one help her drive, she'd probably stop overnight somewhere near the Kansas border.

He calculated her driving time, knowing she'd never go over fifty-five miles an hour in that old car with her children on board. And traveling with three little girls meant numerous stops at restrooms along the interstate.

If he hurried and drove slightly over the speed limit, he had a good chance of catching up with her before she stopped anywhere to spend the night. But if he didn't catch her by then. . . Well, he didn't want to think about that.

ta

The old station wagon labored across I-70, leaving a trail of gray smoke in its wake while three excited girls sang songs, giggled, teased each other, and colored in coloring books. A precious baby boy slept peacefully in the infant seat Hildy and Anna had given her as a gift. But things were not so well for the woman seated behind the steering wheel. She was driving with a broken heart. Each mile marker along I-70 took her one mile further from the love of her life—Bart Ryan.

"Are we there yet, Mama?" little Zana asked from her place in the backseat. "I have to go to the bathroom."

"Not yet. It's a long way to Wichita. Zana, we've already stopped at two restrooms, can't you wait?" Trish asked with a heavy sigh. She wanted to make Colby, Kansas, and find a cheap motel and get settled in before dark. "We'll stop at the next roadside park and eat our sandwiches. Try to be patient, okay?"

"Why'd we have to leave Cedar Ridge, Mama?" Kerel asked as she tucked little Jake's blanket under his chubby chin. "I liked it there. Didn't you like it?"

"Oh, yes, honey. I liked it. I hated to leave as much as you did. But we couldn't stay." Trish stared nervously in the rearview mirror as two eighteen-wheelers barreled up behind her and passed one behind the other.

"But why?" Kari questioned from her place in the backseat.

"Your grandfather said it was time for us to move out of the caretaker's cabin."

"Was somebody else gonna move in?" Kari responded, her face the picture of innocence.

"Maybe—he didn't say," she answered carefully, not wanting to let her daughters know they'd been evicted by the man they believed to be their grandfather.

"Well, I don't get it!" Kerel said indignantly. "I think he's a mean old man."

Trish wanted to agree with her aloud, but constrained herself. "Well, maybe we need to pray for him," she suggested instead.

"Is Bart sad because we're leaving?" Zana asked with a

frown as she closed her coloring book and gazed out the window.

Trish blinked hard. "He said he was sad. But I hope he understands that we had to leave, even though we didn't want to." She forced a happy face. "But think how nice it's going to be to get back to Wichita. Remember how sad you were when we moved away? Think how glad your friends'll be to see you again. And you can show them your new baby brother."

"There's the roadside park," Kari shouted as she pointed to the little building surrounded by picnic tables looming up ahead of them. "You said we'd stop. Are we?"

Trish nodded, flipped on the turn signal, and pulled into the access road. The car chugged to a stop along the curb in front of the restrooms and the little family began pulling on their coats. "Kerel, be sure they—"

"I will, Mom. Don't worry," Kerel called as the girls exited the car and ran toward the ladies' room.

"I want to check the oil," Trish shouted, hoping they'd hear her.

She shivered and buttoned the top button on her coat. As she checked the dipstick, the winter winds wrapped themselves around her. Just as she'd suspected, the car was using far more oil than normal and she prayed the two quarts she'd brought with her would be sufficient until they reached Wichita.

&

Bart's eyes scanned every vehicle as he sped down I-70, searching for the old station wagon so familiar to him. He'd been on the road for over two hours with no success. Surely he hadn't somehow passed her somewhere and missed her. Maybe she'd taken a side road. No, he thought, she wouldn't do that. She'd take the shortest route possible—and that was I-70.

He checked the speedometer. Seventy-five miles per hour. If he was actually going that fast, why did it seem like the pickup was crawling? His fingers drummed impatiently on the steering wheel.

A Colorado Highway Patrol car zoomed around him with its lights flashing and he rechecked his speed. *Trish, where are you?*

Then he spotted it! The old station wagon! Parked at the curb in the roadside park, its hood up. *Praise the Lord! I've found her!*

Quickly flipping on the right turn signal, he crossed to the outside lane, barely making the exit, and rushed the truck into the empty space beside the old wagon.

"Trish! Sweetheart! I've found you!" he called as he leaped from the seat and pulled her into his arms, almost before she realized he was there.

❧

"Bart! What are you doing here?" she asked with wide eyes as he smothered her frigid face with kisses.

"I came to take you home, honey. Where you belong!" He hugged her tight and whirled her through the air as others in the parking lot looked on and snickered at their impromptu reunion. "I love you, Trish Taylor! And I want the entire world to know!" he shouted as he smiled at the onlookers. "I love you! I love you! I love you!"

She pressed her index finger to his lips as she smiled into his beaming face. "Shh. Everyone is watching us."

"I don't care. Let them watch."

Trish giggled like a schoolgirl. "Bart, you're crazy!"

"Crazy in love! Oh, Trish, I had to lose you before I realized how much I loved you. I'm so glad I found you."

She pushed him away from her slightly and bowed her head. "Nothing has changed, Bart."

"Oh, yes, it has! We no longer have to worry about Wilmer pulling the Grayson contract out from under me be—"

She gave him an incredulous look. "He did it?"

Bart laughed mischievously. "Nope. I dumped him!"

"You didn't!"

"Oh, but I did. And you know what? I'm glad he's out of our lives. We don't need him, Trish. We have God!" He lifted her from the pavement and flung her around again. "Three children, seven children. It makes no difference to Him. He owns the cattle on a thousand hills. He'll take care of us—you and me—and all our kids. Didn't He say in His Word, 'Blessed is the man whose quiver is full of them'?" He cupped her chin and lifted her face to his. "Sweetheart, I want to have a full quiver!"

"Oh, Bart. Are you sure you're not delirious?" she asked as she stroked her hero's face.

"Look, Kerel. It's Bart!" Kari shouted as she ran from the restroom into the big man's arms.

The other two girls wrapped their arms around him as his long arms encircled them. "I've come to take you home with me."

Kerel looked up sadly. "But we don't have a home anymore. Grandpa said we had to get out of the cabin."

"You'll have a home if your mama'll agree to marry me!" He turned to Trish, took her hand in his, and knelt on one knee on the rough parking lot.

"How about it, Trish? Will you marry me? Be my wife? And allow me to be a father to your children? I promise to love and care for you 'til death us do part."

Trish looked into the adoring eyes of the man to whom she owed so much, yet she knew the love she was feeling was not one of gratitude. It was a deep, passionate love that would last through eternity. "Nine people! You're ready for that? Do you really want to support nine people, Bart Ryan?"

He caressed her hand, then kissed her fingertips, and looked up into her eyes. "No, I don't want to support nine people, Trish."

She reared back in surprise. "But you said—"

"I want to support ten. Or eleven. Or even twelve! I want us to have babies together. Our babies! God will provide."

She bent and kissed his lips tenderly and smiled into his rugged face as her three daughters and several interested spectators stood watching and listening. "Oh, Bart, we might both be crazy, but yes! Oh, yes! I'll marry you! I love you, too! I guess I've always loved you. I just didn't want to admit it. But now I know, God brought us together. I love you, Bart!"

He stood slowly to his feet, her hands wrapped in his. "Let's go home—"

A hungry baby howled from the backseat of the old station wagon, demanding to be fed.

Bart kissed his fiancée on the tip of her nose. "You'd better go feed *our* baby."

ঌ

It was nearly nine o'clock before the pickup pulled into the garage of the Ryan home.

"That guy at the salvage yard thought you were crazy when you paid him two hundred dollars to haul that old station wagon away," Trish commented thoughtfully, remembering the confused look on the man's face.

"Didn't you hear me the first time I told you? I *am* crazy—crazy in love with you. That was money well spent. No way was I gonna let you ride in another vehicle all the way back to Cedar Ridge. I wanted you right where you are now—by my side."

The big man smiled as he checked the backseat of the extended cab and found the three girls sound asleep, all huddled together. He glanced at little Jake, nestled securely in his car seat behind Trish and Bart, then turned his gaze to her.

"You make a beautiful mama," he said with adoration.

Trish felt the color rise in her cheeks as she touched his hand with her fingertips. "Sure you're not having second thoughts?"

"No way," he said firmly as his finger stroked Jake's cheek gently. "You said yes, remember? We're committed to each other now. No turning back!"

"No turning back," she repeated as she smiled up into his face. "I love you, Bart Ryan."

Bart pulled Trish close and whispered in her ear, "I love you, too, my dandelion bride!"

A Letter To Our Readers

Dear Reader:

In order that we might better contribute to your reading enjoyment, we would appreciate your taking a few minutes to respond to the following questions. We welcome your comments and read each form and letter we receive. When completed, please return to the following:

Fiction Editor
Heartsong Presents
PO Box 719
Uhrichsville, Ohio 44683

1. Did you enjoy reading *Dandelion Bride* by Joyce Livingston?
   ❑ Very much! I would like to see more books by this author!
   ❑ Moderately. I would have enjoyed it more if

   _____

   _____

   _____

2. Are you a member of **Heartsong Presents**? ❑ Yes ❑ No
   If no, where did you purchase this book? _____

   _____

3. How would you rate, on a scale from 1 (poor) to 5 (superior), the cover design? _____

4. On a scale from 1 (poor) to 10 (superior), please rate the following elements.

   ____ Heroine   ____ Plot
   ____ Hero   ____ Inspirational theme
   ____ Setting   ____ Secondary characters

5. These characters were special because?_____

_____

_____

6. How has this book inspired your life?_____

_____

_____

7. What settings would you like to see covered in future
   Heartsong Presents books? _____

_____

_____

8. What are some inspirational themes you would like to see
   treated in future books? _____

_____

_____

9. Would you be interested in reading other **Heartsong
   Presents** titles?   ❏ Yes   ❏ No

10. Please check your age range:
   ❏ Under 18   ❏ 18-24
   ❏ 25-34   ❏ 35-45
   ❏ 46-55   ❏ Over 55

Name_____

Occupation _____

Address _____

City_____ State_____ Zip_____

Alaskan
MIDNIGHT

4 stories in 1

Four women head to Juneau, Alaska, hoping to stitch a new section in their life quilts—a more beautiful section without the tearstains of the past.

Author Joyce Livingston blends the charm of quilting, the drama of the Alaskan landscape, and the thrill of romance into four modern stories of faith and healing.

Historical, paperback, 464 pages, 5 ³/₁₆"x 8"

❤ ❤ ❤ ❤ ❤ ❤ ❤ ❤ ❤ ❤ ❤ ❤ ❤ ❤ ❤ ❤ ❤ ❤ ❤

❤ ❤ ❤ ❤ ❤ ❤ ❤ ❤ ❤ ❤ ❤ ❤ ❤ ❤ ❤ ❤ ❤ ❤ ❤

Heartsong

CONTEMPORARY ROMANCE IS CHEAPER BY THE DOZEN!

Any 12 Heartsong Presents titles for only $27.00*

Buy any assortment of twelve *Heartsong Presents* titles and save 25% off of the already discounted price of $2.97 each!

*plus $2.00 shipping and handling per order and sales tax where applicable.

HEARTSONG PRESENTS TITLES AVAILABLE NOW:

(If ordering from this page, please remember to include it with the order form.)

Presents